Richard Carpenter's

Robin of Sherwood

THE SORCERER'S INCANTATION

I0551988

Richard Carpenter's Robin of Sherwood
The Sorcerer's Incantation
By Jennifer Ash, Paul Birch, and
Paul Kane (from an idea by Jennifer
Ash and Barnaby Eaton-Jones)

Published in 2024 by
Chinbeard Books

in association with
Oak Tree Books
oaktreebooks.uk

Editors: Barnaby Eaton-Jones & Jennifer Ash
Range Consultant: Harriet Whitehouse

Cover shows Richard O'Brien as Gulnar, with
Clive Mantle as Little John, Nickolas Grace
as the Sheriff, Robert Addie as Gisburne
and Claire Toeman as Meg.

Richard Carpenter's

ROBIN OF SHERWOOD

THE SORCERER'S INCANTATION

by
Jennifer Ash,
Paul Birch & Paul Kane

A Chinbeard Books / Oak Tree Books Original

This story is set during Series 3,
two months after *Cromm Cruac*
and before *The Betrayal*.

1: LITTLE JOHN

By Paul Kane

It was a beautiful day in the forest.

The sun cut through the branches of the trees, radiating warmth in spite of the lateness of the year. That usually signalled a harsh winter. But, as with everything else here, they'd deal with that situation when they came to it. Or, more usually, when they were in the midst of it.

John Little—more commonly known for a long time now as 'Little John'—strode through the green, one hand on his trusty staff, the other holding the hand of a woman who had once asked him why they called him 'Little', with a cheeky smile on her face and a mischievous glint in her eye.

The towering giant glanced across to see her now, taking in her pretty face. The dark blonde hair, which—in certain lights—took on a reddish hue, framing those features he knew so well: those big, innocent eyes, high cheekbones and full lips. The face of the woman he cared so much about. He thought back to those days when Meg had first teased him about his moniker, inside her hut, where she lived in Wickham. Ahh, Wickham. A home from their Sherwood home. The village that had become so entwined with the legend of Robin Hood and his outlaw friends. A place they had protected and which, in turn, had protected them; and even hidden them in the past.

It had been very early on when he'd first met Meg, back when Robin of Loxley had been their leader. John had snuck off at every opportunity he could, on the pretext of fishing—which had fooled nobody, especially when he used to come back with no fish, but he couldn't help himself. He'd been drawn to Meg even then.

At first, he'd viewed it as just a bit of harmless fun—and assumed it had been the same for her. But he had to admit to feeling a twinge of jealousy when she'd asked questions like, 'Is he really as handsome as they say?'—about the legendary Robin, of course. Alongside that pang of jealousy, there was also a guarded caution at the thought that the only reason Meg might be with him was because of his connection to that man. Someone who'd taken on the mantle of Herne's Son, protector of the innocent.

But, in his heart, John knew this wasn't really the reason. Naturally, she was fascinated with his life in Sherwood, and he'd joke with her about how he and the others could make themselves invisible to avoid capture.

'Geddaway!' was her response, whilst still believing him a little and asking for a demonstration. It hadn't been a lie—they could all make themselves 'invisible', but only in the forest. Blending in with their surroundings, concealing themselves up trees. They had to, because every single one of them had a price on their heads. Their wolfs' heads.

It had been around that time Meg had first brought up the notion of making things more permanent—their relationship not as casual as maybe he'd thought. 'If I did live in the forest, would you marry me? Go on, say you would!'

John had been taken aback by that, frightened but at the same time he'd be lying if he said the notion didn't appeal to him. Sadly, he hadn't thought about the consequences; it had taken Robin spelling it out to John on his return from seeing Meg one day: '*You* can vanish into Sherwood, the people of Wickham *can't!*'

It had been during that business with Alan-a-Dale, the lovesick minstrel. They'd helped him reunite with his one, true love Mildred, rescuing her from a fate *worse* than death… being married to the Sherrif. And the couple had gone off together to live happily ever after.

By putting those people of Wickham in danger, though, he'd learned a valuable lesson. John began to wonder if there was ever to be a 'happy ever after' for himself and Meg? He had a calling, a purpose. To defend those who couldn't defend themselves—he'd always hated bullies.

It went right back to when he was little… *actually* Little John. Tiny he'd been, as a child. Picked on mercilessly by the bigger boys, he'd come home covered in mud and bruises, much to the chagrin of his mother—his father very rarely around. That had all stopped when John got older, and bigger. *A lot* bigger. Not only had he been able to fight back, but also he could help the other, smaller, children those bullies targeted. Such values had been instilled in him from an early age, and he'd never forgotten.

Perhaps he could no more live the simple life

Meg wanted him to, than she could as an outlaw in Sherwood.

Things had cooled off after that, they'd had to. And when Robin of Loxley had been killed...

The loss of hope, the arguments. The scattering of the 'Merry Men' that were such a part of him. John had retreated back to his old home of Hathersage in Derbyshire, taking Much the Miller's son with him. Licking their wounds really, trying to forget their lives as outlaws by going back to what John had once been, a shepherd. He'd thought about visiting Meg even then, maybe asking her to come with him now he was 'free'. But he was also a broken man, not the easy-going Little John she'd once known. He hadn't meant to abandon her, as his father so often did with his mother when times were hard, especially towards the end when she'd got sick. It had just happened. And John told himself she'd be better off without him anyway. Believed it as well... sometimes.

Then, a year later, Tuck had come to them with a stranger in tow. A man with long, golden hair. As fair as Robin of Loxley's had been dark. The one Herne had chosen to take that Robin's place—as if anyone ever could!—the person who'd both saved them and abandoned them too.

'It means trouble, does this. I can smell it,' John had warned Much.

Something borne out by the fact that the man had sniped: 'Little John? Little brain more like.' Goading him, using a play on his name this time to provoke him rather than gladden his heart.

They say that you never truly know a man until you've fought him. And during that 'fight' with the quarterstaffs, an attempt by Robert of Huntingdon not only to bring John back into the fold, but to prove himself as a potential leader, the giant liked to think he got the measure of this newcomer. Robert may have learned his 'tricks' with the staff from a guard in his castle, but the bravery and the courage had been all his own. This fellow was someone he'd quickly warmed to, particularly when he saw how hard he tried to gather the others, even engaging Scarlet in a fist-fight—not many men had lived to tell that tale after such a thing! How Robert was willing to sacrifice himself for Marion, a prisoner of Owen of Clun and his sorcerer Gulnar's black magic.

It wasn't long before John found himself slipping and calling this man 'Robin', a good while before the others finally did. And though no one could ever replace his dead friend—nothing's really forgotten, it never was—John found a bond building with this former nobleman. A strong bond, one that—more often than not—saw them having late night talks about the way Robert... *Robin* felt about Marion. The way she felt about *him*.

'She feels the same way, John—the way I feel about her. I know it.' That had been something she'd said to him apparently, if she loved him the way he wanted there would be no need for words.

'It's not easy. She just needs time, lad,' John would say to him, clapping Robin on the shoulder.

The more he saw of that relationship, the hesitant path of two steps forward and three steps back that Marion and Robin repeatedly trod, the more John began to think about Meg. And the more he would talk to his friend, sharing their heartfelt secrets.

'I've been to visit her,' John told him one evening by the firelight, the others fast asleep after a large meal of Venison and several mugs of wine. 'Y'know, in Wickham. Meg.'

Robin paused before sipping his own wine, then asked: 'And how did that go?'

It had been awkward to begin with, how could it have been anything else? He'd been gone for so long, not just when he left the area—but before that. Putting distance between them in another way.

They soon discovered, however, that there hadn't really been anyone else in their lives. 'There must have been other girls,' Meg had said, looking down mournfully, 'in Hathersage.' She knew he was a red-blooded male, knew how he'd been back when they first took up. But John had simply lifted her chin and shook his head. 'Nobody. Nobody like you.'

It had ended with a gentle kiss, that conversation. A promise to see each other again and see where things took them. 'I don't suppose I need to warn you to be careful, do I?' Robin had said, with that serious look on his face John had grown used to. Then he'd surprised the larger man by giving a little laugh and drinking more wine. 'Not that you'd listen.'

'You sound just like R—' John caught himself, looked over and offered an unspoken apology, though it was hardly needed. Not these days. Robin gave a small shrug. 'I'll be careful,' John said to him.

And he had been, at first. But what had changed things had been that awfulness in Cromm Cruac. The horrific visions and nightmares he'd had about Meg being chased down by soldiers on horseback, run through and left for dead on some field. To be honest, the whole thing still felt like a nightmare he'd had—only they'd all experienced it. Gulnar's dark labours yet again.

Seeing his other friend Will too, with his dead wife Elena; happy, content. Something that had been denied him, and perhaps explained a lot of Scarlet's explosive anger. John had been forced to snap him out of that illusion, for the man's own good, but not before thinking to himself: life is short, hold on to love where you can find it.

It coincided with Meg starting to mention settling down again to John. He knew that's what she dearly wished, and maybe he was starting to think the same way. That a happy ending might be possible someday?

'Oh, I just don't know, Robin. What do *you* think?' He put the question to him when they were out hunting one afternoon.

'I'm probably the last person you should be taking advice from on your love life,' the blond man had answered.

John recalled seeing the way Marion and he had looked at each other on those stones by the stream, after they'd defeated Gulnar once more. When she'd slipped and Robin had caught her. The look they'd briefly shared. They were getting closer and closer with each passing day, but Marion was still holding back. In the future, perhaps...

Yet here was a woman who wanted John, right now. With all of his bad habits and stubborn moods, even after the way he'd treated her before. Not that Meg couldn't be stubborn herself when she wanted to be, couldn't be difficult to be around. She was strong-willed all right, one of the things he adored about her. John wasn't so in love that he was blind to her faults, not at all, it was just that when you *were* in love you accepted everything a person was. Heart and soul. He'd learned that lesson eventually too.

They were all getting older, as well. Thoughts turning to family, to little ones maybe? You only had to look at the way they were with children like Matthew—Edward and Alison's son, who spent time now and again in Sherwood—to see that it had crossed their minds. John's, Robin and Marion's. Perhaps even Much, and even Will. Not Tuck though; *definitely* not Tuck.

The idea of something *more* than this, a life on the run. Constantly looking over your shoulder for Gisburne and his mob. Be a father, but a present father—not constantly abandoning people.

It came down to a choice. One life or the other, more than likely far away. Back in Hathersage again? He did so miss that place when he wasn't there, almost as much as he missed Sherwood when he was away from that. It was as he'd told Robin himself: 'It's not easy.' None of this was.

'No, go on. I want to hear what you think,' John pressed him, out on that hunt.

Robin released a slow breath. 'All right. Well, if you are serious about all this, John, then I'd advise you to spend some days with Meg. Not just a stolen night here or there, but perhaps… a break? A day or two off.'

'A break?' The only days off John had known were due to holydays and celebrations, like the ones they'd had back in Hathersage around Midsummer's Eve, involving Maypoles and games like tug-of-war. Ones where people danced too much, drank too much and inevitably ended up passed out on the ground.

'Just you and Meg.'

'Just me and Meg?' John repeated again.

Robin nodded. 'Change of scenery, getting away. Some people do it.'

'*I* don't,' he answered. John assumed his friend was talking about the rich.

Their leader chuckled. 'It'll be a way of knowing for sure whether you're ready to take the next step. Spend your life with her. Like a practise.'

'A practise?' John shook his head; it was beginning to sound like an echo. Yet he couldn't help saying one last time: 'Just me and Meg?'

11

Robin stopped walking and faced him, smiling and raising an eyebrow. '*Just* you and Meg.'

John smiled back. Then he frowned. 'But what about you lot?'

'I daresay we'll manage,' Robin told him, smile even wider.

'No, I mean what will we tell everyone?' He didn't mind Robin knowing his business, but all he'd get from the likes of Will would be a ragging.

'I'll tell them you're on an errand of mercy,' he said seriously, then chuckled again.

John slapped him on the back. 'Aye. I just might be at that.' They both laughed then. But as the laughter died down, he could have sworn he'd seen something in Robin's eye. A sorrow there, like he'd just set something in motion he might regret. That would come back to bite him. They'd manage without John for a little while, but forever? Now that was a different proposition altogether.

Needless to say, Meg had been thrilled. 'Oh John! What a wonderful idea,' she'd cooed, flinging her arms around him when he told her. 'However did you think of it?'

Stepping back, John shrugged sheepishly, and she hugged him again—barely able to reach around his frame. 'Just me and you,' she said, voice muffled by his side. He could tell what she was thinking: none of the other outlaws in the way; no disturbances.

'Aye lass, just you and me.'

She pulled back. 'Ooh, and I know the perfect place an' all.'

'You do?' asked John, cocking his head.

Meg nodded excitedly. 'Nice and quiet, somewhere I used to play with my cousins when we were children. Somewhere nobody would ever think to look for us.' She didn't need to add, 'In case the others need you, in case there's yet another caper they want to drag you off on.' But that worked both ways, didn't it. If they didn't know where he was, he'd be on his own if he got into trouble and needed help. Not that he was intending to do that, except…

It was something that definitely occurred to John when Meg told him at last where she had in mind for their 'break'.

'Yer what?' John asked, thinking he'd misheard her.

'The caves,' Meg said again. 'Below Nottingham Castle.'

John opened his mouth and closed it, then opened it again. Meg giggled, in that way that she did—sweet and impish at the same time. 'But—'

'Just think about it, John. Spending time alone, right under the Sherrif's nose… and he won't know a thing about it!'

John rubbed his bearded chin. The idea was starting to appeal to him, particularly if the caves Meg meant were as secluded as she said. 'I promise, we'll be totally alone,' she said, beaming.

So John gave another shrug, and they made plans to set off the very next day.

Which was how they'd come to be on the other side of the forest, walking in the sunshine. John thought back again about how far he'd come, not just on this particular trail, but on this journey altogether. Thought about what might lie ahead.

He realised Meg had said something he'd missed. 'What's that?'

'I said it's not too far now, John… Are you all right?'

'Sorry, lass. I was miles away.'

She looked hurt by that, his mind wandering when he should be with her in the here and now. John gave Meg a big grin and dropped his staff, picking her up as he often did and whirling her around. Then kissed her. Meg giggled once more.

When he put her down, John bent and picked a flower—one of the few remaining red campions this late in the season (which were actually purple in colour)—before placing it behind her ear.

'Beautiful,' he said. 'The flower *and* you.'

Meg batted his chest. 'Charmer.'

John looked beyond her. 'Not too far, you say. Come on then,' he enthused, retrieving his staff. 'Let's go. I can't wait!'

Meg hadn't been wrong.

They'd barely been walking half an hour when John spotted the rocks she'd talked about. There they were, in the shadow of Nottingham Castle itself. The sight of that place gave him pause for thought. Recalling the times they'd had to break in, the occasions they'd been taken prisoner.

The home of their enemy.

John shivered involuntarily. Meg took his hand and pulled him along, taking no notice herself. 'Invisible, remember?' she whispered to him, as if she was able to read his thoughts—those very memories he'd been reliving back there on the hike. Once he couldn't see the castle itself, though, he brightened up. Meg tickled him, and they laughed together.

Both looking forward to the time they'd spend in each other's company. Robin had definitely had a point; the change of scenery was doing them good. Neither Sherwood nor Wickham, not even Hathersage.

They paused and kissed again, John holding Meg tight. 'I love you,' she said in hushed tones.

'An' I love you.'

Another laugh, more tugging on his arm, and she pointed at the cave entrance. 'There it is, John! Told you! Come on.'

'You were right, lass.'

She was desperate for their break to begin in earnest, and John couldn't say he blamed her. Yet the cautious side of his nature remained, the part of him that had lived in the forest as a wanted man all this time. 'You go inside, Meg, I'll just make sure no one followed us.'

'Oh, John! It'll be fine. Let's get in the cave. We'll be safe in there.' Meg had hold of him, pulling him closer to her. They were practically entwined, wrapped around each other and stumbling, sniggering and tittering like youngsters. Like Meg and her cousins when they'd played here as children.

So wrapped up in each other, that they barely noticed what was right in front of them. Not even the smell, a cloying stench that suddenly wormed its way into his throat and burnt the sides. Hadn't smelt *this* trouble, had he?

John cursed himself silently, for letting his guard slip. He took in the scene ahead of him, blinking—taking in the shapes there, the surroundings.

There was a fire, fierce, belching out flames that were red in colour and shooting upwards; illuminating walls that had been decorated with an odd assortment of rugs and cloaks, which gave it the appearance of being a living thing. A beast crowding in on them.

But that wasn't all. Shelves had been fixed to the walls as well, wooden shelves all around them, holding up jars and bottles filled with strange-coloured liquids, small bones and skulls dotted here and there. Weird objects, ornaments made from twigs and stone, creepers and plants snaking around them. Nothing evaded John's keen eye now.

A space had been created in the middle of the floor, mess and litter—including what looked like a cooking cauldron of some kind, its chains hanging limply as if its usual home was above the fire—shoved and swept off to the sides. To make way for something that was grey and wet and appeared sticky; a substance that looked very much like clay, which was... moving.

Kneeling next to this with their hands plunged inside the grey sludge, were two figures. John didn't want to believe what his eyes were telling him, but there they were, right in front of him! One was a blond man, with hair as light as Robin's in fact, but whose features were twisted and sour. His wide, staring eyes, usually full of hatred, seemed dulled somehow though, like he was half-asleep. Next to him was an older man; he might have been wearing a hat, but to John, there was no disguising those teeth that glistened in the firelight, or the tongue which darted rapidly in and out with each strange word he was mouthing.

Gisburne and Gulnar!

What in Herne's name were they doing here, and why were they *together*? It was almost as if, by thinking about them on the trail here, John had conjured them up. Indeed, he did wonder for a moment or two, whether he was simply imagining them; his memories lingering like phantoms after a bad dream.

Bad dream? These two were the very embodiment of bad dreams, especially that demented sorcerer—the bringer himself of nightmares and horrific visions. John gaped at him, seeing the damage that man was recovering from. The burns on the face, around the eyes, though healing, were still there—a consequence of Marion throwing holy water from Thornton Abbey in his face. She'd poured it into the stream first to destroy the wicked god he was resurrecting, then used it on his servant… to great effect. Gulnar had fallen into the water himself, shrieking in agony. They'd thought him dead, yet here he was. John should have known you could never really kill evil incarnate.

They locked eyes, and Gulnar recognised him—just as he had the sorcerer. John could feel that cold, hard stare boring into him, trying to overpower him. To work its magic. He looked away, not giving him the opportunity.

'Grab them!' Gulnar ordered his cohort, who leapt up, his uniform covered in wet clay. Meg was the closest to him, and so he took hold of her first. As shocked as she was at finding *anyone* here, Meg struggled to free herself from the man's grasp, the flower falling from behind her ear. She yelled and screamed; shouts that echoed throughout the cavernous environment.

John, for his part, stepped forward and swung the quarterstaff he was holding. Suddenly in the midst of the unexpected again. But he knew that if he was going to stop this, he had to incapacitate the sorcerer. If Gisburne was following his commands, he wasn't dazed so much as bewitched. John had seen this before, first with Marion when Gulnar had tried to make her more compliant for his former master, Owen. Then with Nasir, at Cromm Cruac— when he didn't even recognise them, and just kept mouthing words in his mother tongue, Arabic.

With a swift prod, John knocked his enemy over onto the lump of greyness—and had he imagined it, or did he hear that clay cry out as if in pain? 'Gulnar!' he shouted, saying the name out loud now. Before being distracted by what was happening with the women he loved, still attempting to escape. 'Gisburne!' John bellowed with a snarl, promptly turning the staff on him and raising it for another blow.

There was a noise behind them all, which suddenly made them freeze.

'Gisburne!! Where the hell are you?' The voice drifted in from outside, a familiar voice with an unmistakably nasty edge to it.

The Sheriff! thought John. *Now* he's *here too!*

Far from being alone, being safe—in a spot where nobody would ever think to look for them, as Meg had promised—he appeared to be surrounded by foes on all sides.

Just him and Meg. Meg and him… Hardly!

A trap of some kind, most likely. His first instinct was to batter Gisburne and flee with Meg, of course. But he couldn't chance being caught in Gulnar's gaze or being hemmed in by de Rainault, and whatever men he had out there. Most important of all, however, he couldn't risk Meg getting hurt in whatever fight came next—the image of her running across that field and being brought down still fresh in his mind.

You're abandoning her again…

No. He needed time to think, time to figure out his next step. It's what Robin would do. 'I'll be back, Meg,' he said in hushed tones.

Then he retreated, rushing back out the way he came.

John half-stumbled, half-fell over the Sherrif as he exited.

He appeared to be alone, as far as John could see—even if he hadn't been, John had the little toad by the scruff of the neck; ready and more than willing to use him as a human shield or a bargaining tool, whichever way worked best.

21

John dragged him from the cave and towards the undergrowth. 'Unhand me, you villain!' the Sheriff protested, then threw back his head to call out: 'Help me, he—'

Swiftly, John clamped a hand over the man's mouth, something he always felt like doing whenever he encountered him. He suspected many others felt exactly the same way. 'Be quiet!' he snapped.

Glancing around, John found an overgrown spot where he could throw down the Sherrif and still keep one eye on the cave. He shoved the end of his staff in the man's face. 'Call out for help again, and—'

The Sheriff crawled backwards, hitting a tree-trunk and holding up his hands. 'All right, all right. I understand.'

Looking about him again, John asked: 'What are you doing here?'

'What am I doing here?' replied the man furiously. 'What am *I doing* here..? That's my castle up there, you imbecile. These are my lands!'

He'd meant, more accurately, what was the Sheriff doing here *alone*? Or had John been asking, what was he up to with Gisburne and Gulnar? If they were all working together, it could only spell trouble… quite literally in the case of Gulnar. But John just shook his head in exasperation.

'I could ask you the same thing,' the Sheriff said, his right eye turning to a slit and his other one bulging. 'What's your business with Gisburne and that old man back in the cave, John Little of Hathersage?'

John touched his chest. '*My* business?'

Didn't like people knowing his business...

The Sheriff nodded. 'And where are the rest of your... *associates*?' He said it with such disdain, it was like he was trying to spit out a hair from his mouth. Loathing: he loathed them all. Much had asked him why, back when they'd found de Rainault wandering through Sherwood in rags, kicked out of that castle he now proclaimed as his own and usurped by a new Sheriff: the sadistic Philip Mark. They'd tied him up in their camp and he'd answered: 'I hate you for what you are—and what you stand for. There's a difference isn't there. You're outlaws, thieves, murderers; but you stand for freedom, for justice, for the people... What I hate most about you is the legend that surrounds you... Peasants and simpletons, and yet the people look up to you. And even respect you.' He had sounded almost envious, because the inhabitants of Nottingham and the surrounding areas loathed him just as much as he did the outlaws.

23

Yet Robin had been the one who'd struck upon the truth of the matter, as always. Evidenced by the way the Sheriff was quivering even now—though to be fair, a huge, bearded man *was* standing over him, threatening his life. 'But you haven't told us the real reason why you hate us so. You're afraid of us,' Robin had stated flatly.

Afraid enough to work with a practitioner of the dark arts? No, the Sheriff was still waiting for an answer—as confused as he was scared. Just like John. 'I have no business with them.' He gritted his teeth. 'I was going about my *own* business, when I came upon them.'

'Lies!' the Sheriff spat again.

'Why would I lie about it? It's your man who was with Gulnar, Sheriff!'

'Who?' demanded de Rainault.

'Did you not recognise him? The man back there in the cave?'

The Sheriff shook his head.

'You remember Owen of Clun, surely?'

'Of course!' John could see his unlikely companion thinking back, recalling the brute. 'That Welsh oaf who attacked Richard of Leaford!'

'Aye, when he kidnapped Marion.'

The Sheriff sneered; he couldn't care less about

Richard's daughter. Indeed, he'd made a mint out of cheating Sir Richard by promising men that fled when confronted by Clun's forces. That was always the bottom line with de Rainault: money. 'What of it? The man's dead. I heard your *precious* leader killed him.'

'Aye, Clun's dead all right. The portcullis of his keep fell on top of 'im. *That*,' said John, thumbing back towards the cave, 'was his sorcerer, Sheriff!'

The man laughed bitterly. 'Sorcerer! Have you taken leave of your senses? You might believe in all that superstitious nonsense but—'

'It's not nonsense,' John cut in with a growl.

'This coming from a man who worships a pagan spirit in the forest.'

'Not another word,' said John, jamming his staff in his enemy's face again. 'Herne's real,' he argued. 'And so are Gulnar's powers. I've seen 'em for myself.'

In spite of the warning, de Rainault laughed. 'Of course you have.'

'He can resurrect the dead. He can make you see things that aren't there. And,' John continued, 'he can take control of your mind.'

The Sheriff considered this last part for a minute. John could see that he'd struck a nerve. Remembering how Gisburne had been behaving back in the cave, the outlaw asked, 'Has Guy been acting strangely?'

De Rainault remained silent, so John prompted him again.

'He's been... nice,' the Sheriff admitted grudgingly, and with as much disdain as he'd shown John's band. 'Distracted, grinning like an idiot. Happy! If I didn't know better, and if I thought he might be able to actually feel emotions, I'd say he was in love.'

'The only person Gisburne's in love with is 'imself,' replied John, almost throwing in 'like you' for good measure. 'But no, *nice*. That really doesn't sound like Guy.'

'He's not been responding to my usual barbs, just shrugs them off.' De Rainault screwed up his face. 'I ask you, where's the fun in that?'

'Where indeed,' said John sarcastically.

'He's apparently been treating the servants courteously, too. Thanking them!'

'How disgusting.'

'Don't mock me,' cautioned the Sheriff, bristling and half-rising.

'Or what?' said John, brandishing his staff again.

The man settled down, groaning. 'It's why I was following him in the first place, if you must know.'

Ah, so that was it, thought John. Certainly explained why de Rainault was on his own. He wondered then if Guy had gone behind this man's back and sought out Gulnar himself. After all, Gisburne was always trying to get one over on his master—not to mention them. Perhaps he thought an alliance might bring down Robin Hood once and for all, might even win him the title of Sheriff? If so, Gisburne had woefully underestimated the sorcerer, just like de Rainault appeared to be doing.

'So, you accept that Gisburne might well be under the influence of Gulnar, then?'

'I accept no such thing!' But the Sheriff's expression said otherwise.

'Marion almost wed Owen of Clun because of something similar, that's how strong his powers are.'

'Powers of persuasion, perhaps,' countered the Sheriff. 'Is it not also possible that the Lady Wolfshead just wanted to marry someone with a castle, with an estate?'

'If she'd wanted that, she'd have done it long ago,' answered John, 'and chosen someone less... ruthless.' No, Marion followed her heart—always had. It was part of the problem with Robin right now, her heart belonged in two places: the past and the present. 'Besides, no amount of convincing could make Gisburne treat servants that way. Make him act "happy".'

'Very well, assuming you're right. That this… Gulnar has a kind of hold over Gisburne, what does he want with him?'

John scratched his beard. 'I don't know. But it probably involves taking his revenge on Robin, that was at the root of it last time.' John explained what had happened at Cromm Cruac, ignoring the occasional 'hah!' from the Sheriff who no doubt dismissed it all as more superstitious nonsense. 'We left Gulnar for dead, but he's obviously been recovering here. In that cave. And planning his next move.'

'Which is?'

'How should *I* know?' John grunted in frustration. 'I'll bet you anything it has something to do with that clay thing, mind.'

'Clay?' said the Sheriff.

'They were sculpting something,' John explained. 'Didn't you see? And the way that clay… It seemed to be moving, alive.'

Another cackle from de Rainault, but there was a nervous tinge to it. 'You said yourself that lunatic could make you see things that aren't there. If you believe that, then—'

'This was something else, Sheriff. Trust me.'

'Trust you? I'd just as soon trust a snake.'

'I feel exactly the same way, but if we're going to get to the bottom of this. If we're going to stop them, then...'

'What?' De Rainault still didn't understand what John was driving at. That they both had a common enemy.

'We're going to have to work together,' John said, putting it plainly.

'Outrageous!' spluttered the Sheriff—both his eyes turning to slits now. 'I will not be a party to this, working with you and your rabble.'

'You've done it before,' John reminded him. 'Sort of. When you had to. When you showed us those secret tunnels under the castle.'

'Tunnels I've since sealed up, I assure you!'

'I believe you, Sheriff. But this time, there *aren't* any others. It's just me. Robin and the rest of my friends are miles away. By the time I fetched them, Meg might be—'

'Meg?' asked the Sheriff. 'Ah, there *was* someone here with you—was there not? I thought I glimpsed a female.'

John looked down woefully. 'Aye.'

'A female you care about, then.' Gisburne and the Sheriff might not have had emotions as such, but John definitely did… and he found it hard to conceal them. 'A woman you abandoned.'

John ground his teeth, bending and grabbing de Rainault by the front of his tunic. 'I did *not* abandon her!'

'W-Whatever you say,' choked the smaller man.

John slowed his breathing, reminded himself that he needed this weasel. That he couldn't do this alone. That even with two of them, the odds were not great. 'You want Gisburne back, don't you.'

De Rainault hesitated far longer than he probably should have, before nodding. 'Back the way he was, at least. Better the devil you know.'

'I want Meg back too. And we both need to stop Gulnar, whatever he's doing. Agreed?'

The Sheriff concurred with a long sigh. 'So, what do you propose we do?'

John looked back over towards the cave. 'I don't see that we have any choice,' he replied. 'We wait.'

They crept closer and hid at the edges of the foliage.

In sight of the cave, ready to spring into action when they spotted movement. There was no use rushing back in there, as John had pointed out, because they'd be expecting that. *Gulnar* would be expecting it—and ready for them. In a confined space like that, they'd be done for. When you were hunting, sometimes the best thing to do was just wait for your prey to emerge and come to you.

But waiting wasn't something de Rainault appeared to relish. He shifted about as they laid there on their bellies. Wriggling and tutting, moaning about his clothes even after John had warned him about making too much noise. The man wouldn't last five minutes hiding out in Sherwood.

Then suddenly he turned to John. 'This Meg of yours, I think I remember her.'

John said nothing.

'It was a long time ago, and I think I was very drunk on wine. But I... I remember her coming to the castle, to plead for the lives of some villagers. Yes, that's right. I'd put a price of a hundred marks on each of their heads. She came and said she could help me catch you bandits if I pardoned her community. Was bawling her eyes out—stupid wench!'

John grimaced, remembering. That was the very occasion he'd been thinking about, the one when Robin of Loxley had warned him of the dangers of seeing Meg. It had been his fault, all of it.

'I didn't believe her, of course! Threw her out, if I recall.' Part of a plan that hadn't worked, so they'd been forced to think up another. Thankfully, the newly rescued Mildred had given them a necklace the sheriff had given her so they could pay the money.

I have a treasure beyond riches, love conquers all.

John cast his mind back to the wedding ceremony in Sherwood, Alan and Mildred getting wed and Meg nudging him, urging them to be next. Maybe—

'There!' said the Sheriff, his voice rising.

John was about to tell him to be quiet again, when he saw what the man was pointing at. 'Gisburne… And he looks like he's on his own. This is our chance, come on!' He rose up, dragging de Rainault with him.

Sir Guy still looked lost, grinning that same grin the Sherrif had talked about. Wandering as if not really knowing what to do next. Although he did seem a little more aware of his surroundings, gazing around him at the cave entrance with a frown on his face, as if not knowing how he'd come to be there.

'He's fighting back, fighting the enchantment,' John said. 'Quick, grab him!'

'I don't really— I'm not one for getting my hands dirty.'

John moaned and headed towards Gisburne himself, vaguely aware of the Sheriff trailing him. The soldier saw John and began to reach for his sword, yet still appeared bewildered. A reflex action, which John needed to put paid to. He slammed Gisburne's fingers with his staff. 'Don't even think about it, Gisburne... What's happening to Meg?'

'Meg?'

'Oh for God's sake, Gisburne.' It was only now that the Sheriff came out from behind John, rounding him. 'What has got into you?'

'Nothing. I'm...'

'It's not nothing!' John was looking in every direction, wary of standing out in the open too long—preparing for any attacks. 'Meg is in there with one of the evilest men in the world and *you* are helping him!'

'Helping... I'm...' The fellow's words seemed to dry up, and he looked from John to the Sheriff strangely. It reminded John of how Nas had been when they couldn't get through to him. 'You two... you don't normally help each other... do you?'

The Sheriff was quick to agree. 'No we do *not*!'

With a sideways look, John commented: 'Here and now we *are* helping each other, but just while you and Meg are in danger, Gisburne.'

'*Me* and Meg?'

De Rainault drew closer, peering at his underling. 'You were right, he has been possessed.'

'Aye, and with that one in there, a simple knocking on the head isn't going to bring him out of it. Let's get him into the trees.'

Like he'd had a knock on the head already, Gisburne feebly let himself be led back towards the woodland. 'If you betray me Sheriff, then Robin will see you dead,' John reminded his unlikely comrade. 'Do you understand? Dead. Both of you.'

'You've made your point.' De Rainault switched his attention to Sir Guy. 'Why are *you* covered in clay, Gisburne, and what in Hell's name is Clun's sorcerer doing in one of my caves?!' The Sheriff had apparently accepted that was what Gulnar was, thought John.

'Sorcerer?'

'Yes!'

'I'm helping the old man. I don't know about a sorcerer.'

'Gisburne, the only person you have ever helped in your whole life is yourself.' De Rainault jabbed a finger into Sir Guy's chest. 'Now talk to me.'

'I just got a hermit some water and herbs—oh, and some clay. That's all.'

John pulled a face, acutely aware that the sound

of their conversation was carrying. 'Will you keep your voice down!?'

Gisburne's tone softened. 'If it will help.'

The Sheriff had been right, this friendlier version of Sir Guy was just wrong, and deeply disturbing. 'The clay was moving,' John insisted.

'Moving?' De Rainault looked uncertain, yet in the end he still shrugged this off. 'You haven't been possessed as well have you?'

'I tell you, Sheriff, that clay on the cave floor, it was moving like it was alive.'

John clamped a hand on Gisburne's shoulder, and the soldier cast his eyes back towards the cave. 'You… I have met you before somewhere.'

John caught the eyeroll the Sheriff gave him. 'Well done, Gisburne. Sharp as an arrow as usual.'

'What does Gulnar want with Meg?' John lowered his grip to Gisburne's sword-arm, still preventing him from drawing it.

'He's practising.'

Like a practise…

'I beg your pardon?' The Sheriff retreated a few steps.

'Revenge…' Gisburne blinked a few times, gave a little shake of his head. It was as if things were coming back to him slowly, in bits.

'But Meg hasn't done anything to him!' John's words tumbled out. 'It was bad enough when Gulnar tortured me with dreams of seeing her killed. Over and over I saw her run down by…' He couldn't help himself, he rounded on de Rainault. '…*your* men. But the only thing Meg has ever done that could be seen as wrong in your eyes is love me, and I will not see her punished for that!'

'Meg of Wickham…'

'You do remember her, don't you, Gisburne?' That was good and bad news, as far as John was concerned. 'She lives in Wickham with Edward and the others.'

'Wickham? Trouble… we've had trouble there.'

'Damn right we've had trouble there, Gisburne! Him for a start.' The Sheriff pointed at John, and if his finger had been a crossbow bolt he would have fallen down stone dead. 'Don't you remember? You've been humiliated there so many times, that surely…'

'Humiliated…' Gisburne's rage returned all at once, and John had no choice but to relieve him of his sword now—tossing it away—before yanking both his arms behind his back. '…That's what you do to me. That's why I was leaving… I was leaving…' Guy was staring fiercely at the Sheriff. 'You threw wine at me and… I went off to think. There was an old man who…'

'That was Gulnar!!'

The out of place smile returned to his face, as Gisburne switched back from furious to placid once more. 'Umm… yes. I'm his deputy now. I'm going to be his son.'

'His son?' asked the Sheriff, gazing in disbelief at John.

'One of his sons. He has seen it.'

John bit his bottom lip so hard he almost drew blood; this was far worse than he'd thought. 'Gulnar does see things. Worse, he can make *you* see things, things that aren't real. And he *hates* Robin… If he is planning on making Gisburne his son, as the sort of opposite to Robin being Herne's Son…'

'That is a situation I do not want to consider,' admitted de Rainault.

'Nor do I!' John was restless, his thoughts turning to his sweetheart again. 'I have to get Meg out of there. Or rather…' Hauling Gisburne up by his collar, he let out a low roar. '…*You* are going to go back in there and fetch her.'

'Gulnar said not to come back,' he argued, and gave an apologetic shrug, grinning that same inane grin. 'But I'll see him again. I'll be useful again.'

'You haven't been useful in years.'

'Shut up, Sheriff… If Gulnar has finished with Gisburne, here, then the enchantment might wear off soon.'

'I hope so! There's not much more of that smile I can take.' De Rainault snorted. 'Bloody sorcerers. At least when the Baron de Belleme was around he had intelligence and breeding! This one's barking mad.' So, his tolerance and belief in 'nonsense' depended on standing—was that it? Typical, thought John.

'We have to get…' John tensed, sensing movement—his hand shot up to cover Gisburne's mouth in case he should cry out. 'Shh… what was that noise?'

The was a muffled scream and all the men stood stock-still. It was John who roused himself first, dragging his charge out to the edge of the thicket with him. A cry of pain came next, quickly followed by a second scream from the man. Meg, it had to be—fighting back! That was his girl, he thought: strong-willed, stubborn. John beamed proudly, but that smile soon faded when the next scream to come was clearly a woman's.

'We are going to get her. Now!' John snapped, silently praying for Herne to protect his Meg.

'We? But Gisburne was going?' There was a hitch in the Sheriff's voice.

'Look at him! He hasn't got a clue what's going on, and if it's all the same to you, I'd rather not wait around for him to remember who I am or who he is.'

'I bet you wouldn't!'

Now John ripped off Gisburne's belt and tied his hands with it. 'Come on, Sheriff!' They'd started this together; they were going to finish it the same way.

Leaving Gisburne behind, John made the Sheriff go in front—thereby ensuring he came with him.

They entered cautiously, but when John spotted Meg's prone form on the floor that soon changed. Speeding forwards, he hefted his quarterstaff. The edge of it swept across the back of Gulnar's bald head, and he fell forwards. There was a yelp and John looked across to see the Sheriff gazing in horror at the clay figure that… that was in the shape of a… a person! A moving person; John had tried to tell him.

There was no use pondering what Gulnar had been doing, however. 'Time to get your hands *really* dirty!' shouted John. 'Smash it, Sheriff! Before Gulnar can recover. Destroy the dark magic!' The Sherrif was still hesitating, so John added as a final incentive: 'Do it! Or I'll tell everyone how we worked together, how you helped a wolf's head!'

That did the trick. Lip curling, the Sheriff tore into the clay, pulling it to pieces, breaking it all up into chunks. There was a whine of 'No' from Gulnar's position, before he slumped at last. Unconscious or dead, it made little difference to John. All he could think about was Meg, lying there on the floor.

He went to her, hadn't abandoned her—but he hadn't been here when it counted either. 'Oh lass, please be all right. Please be alive. I'll do anything you want. I will, I promise.' John cradled her head on his lap, then bent and listened for a breath. There was nothing at first and he feared the worst.

Then he felt it on his cheek, weak but there. He let out a wail of joy mixed with a sob.

'More snivelling,' chuntered the Sherrif as he continued to tear up the clay, stamping on it when it was on the floor. 'I'll do the same with this place that I did with the tunnel,' John heard him muttering, but took little notice. 'Seal it up—with him inside it!' He was stabbing an angry finger at Gulnar's body.

John didn't care, but felt like it was probably time to get out of there before the Sheriff's men finally arrived and he decided to imprison them inside as well. Make damned sure John never spoke a word of this to anyone.

Leaving his staff behind, John gathered Meg up in his arms and started towards the doorway.

'And where do you think *you're* going?' yelled the Sheriff after him. 'Stop! I'll have you arrested! I'll see you hanged! Stop!'

John did stop, paused at any rate. But not because of what the Sheriff had said. He spotted the flower he'd given Meg, trampled on the floor of the cave—but still intact.

John stooped and snagged it between his fingers, then left as fast as he could.

John headed back into the forest.

He ran as far away from that place as possible. From more memories he'd no doubt be begging to forget. Carried his beloved away, checking on her as he went. Seeing if she was still breathing, her chest going up and down, holding that campion in his hand. Survivors, both of them. John ferried her away until he was certain it was just the two of them.

Just him and Meg. Meg and him.

When he was too tired to go any further, he stopped and set Meg down on a makeshift cushion of leaves and plants. There she slept and he stayed with her, next to her. Holding her hand and holding the flower.

As the giant glanced across now, staring at her pretty face—the dark blonde hair, which in certain lights looked more reddy-brown, framing those features he knew so well: those big, innocent eyes, high cheekbones and full lips; the face of the woman he cared about so much—he thought back… Back to the cave and those final few moments during all the chaos.

Thought about that clay thing in there the Sheriff had broken up and trampled.

'The clay was moving… I tell you, that clay on the cave floor, it was moving like it was alive.'

About how much it had looked like a person. Like a woman, actually. How much it had looked like—

John shook his head. One day he'd piece it all together, figure out what it might have to do with Gulnar's plan—claiming Gisburne as his son, reaping his revenge upon Robin. Maybe even something to do with Marion, about the way they felt for each other..? Was Gulnar even still alive?

Should have known you could never really kill evil incarnate.

Whatever the case, his creation would be buried with him, if the Sherrif had anything to do with it. Just like the men who'd built those secret tunnels for him under the castle.

One day all of this would make sense, John was sure of that, but not now. Now he had more important things to worry about.

Like the obvious truth that Meg had been in danger again, due to the fact they—*he*—had enemies. How he would probably have to make a choice sooner than he thought. About the future, about *their* future: his and Meg's. About the promise he'd made back there, that he'd do anything. That he'd never abandon her again.

'Would you marry me? Go on, say you would!'

A wedding ceremony in Sherwood, Alan and Mildred getting wed and Meg nudging him, urging them to be next.

Perhaps he could no more live the simple life Meg wanted him to, than she could as an outlaw in Sherwood. Sooner or later, there would have to be a choice.

I have a treasure beyond riches, love conquers all.

But would she be all right? that was the question. Gulnar had shown him her death previously in a nightmare, a vision. Had the man, the sorcerer, actually killed her for real this time?

At that moment, Meg's eyelids fluttered. *Herne be praised!* John leaned in closer, said her name softly. Blinking hard, she opened her eyes and winced. 'I… W-Where am I?'

'You're safe,' he informed her. It was the most important thing as far as he was concerned.

'No… no, I mean… *John?*' she said then, as if she'd just realised he was with her.

'I'm here, my love. I'm not going anywhere.'

'John…' Another wince. 'What happened? I don't remember what…'

'It's all right. Don't you worry about that.' Whether her loss of memory was a consequence of Gulnar's enchantments or whatever tussle had been going on before they entered the cave, John didn't know. But maybe it was all for the good. Some memories *are* best forgotten.

'I don't… what happened to me?'

'You just slipped and hit your head, that's all. I'm going to get you back home. Get you well again, my love.'

Meg frowned, then nodded—and winced a final time.

The sun was waning, the beautiful day in the forest was giving way to the night. Always in balance, just like the powers of light and darkness. Like life and death. 'Is it all right if I…' John motioned that he was going to pick her up again and Meg told him it was. But before he did, he gave her the flower, placing it in the palm of her hand. She stared at it, another frown on her face, before offering a little smile.

'One, two…' John slid his massive hands under her and hoisted Meg aloft. She slung her arms around him, head nestled into his chest.

'Just… just don't let go of me, John. Will you?' she said, her voice tiny.

'No lass, I won't.' And he didn't intend to. At some point, when Meg was recovered, there would have to be a decision. Robin had sent him off to make one about it all, whether John felt like he could live with this woman for the rest of his life.

The thing was, John didn't think he could live *without* her. Perhaps that decision would be both of theirs to make, or would it just be Meg's? If it went the way he thought, John doubted that Robin and the others would be happy when he eventually broke it to them—not to begin with anyway.

But he'd never forget his friends, John knew that too—whatever happened. They'd be a part of him, forever.

All of them.

2: GULNAR

By Paul Birch

Death was always a doorway. Gulnar had known that from the beginning. He had found himself, an unwanted seventh child, tied in a sack and thrown into the water by his father. The water was intended to consume him; yet it did not. Death had come close and, as a child, he had seen Death's Door in his almost-final moments. His little foot had stepped across the threshold and his tiny hand had passed through for a brief second. Even a part of his mind had ventured across, and he had seen the beyond.

Seen too much.

Then, unseen hands had pulled him back before he could step fully through. The hands of the river Maun, or of life, or of the gods. Who knew? He didn't. Which was odd, for Gulnar knew more than most. Death, it seemed, wanted him no more than his father did.

He was always an unwanted thing. Unwanted until Owen of Clun had found him and welcomed him into his bloody court. And now that life had been taken and thrown away too and, after its destruction, nobody wanted him to linger there either.

But he would be wanted again. His need—hunger—for revenge would see to that.

Now, stood on the edge of a wheat field, the shadow of Nottingham Castle looming over the distant sun-soaked horizon, Gulnar watched the golden strands of corn sway in the breeze. His stomach churned—the ripened corn, so lush, so good for the people—was the same colour as Robert of Huntingdon's hair.

He felt Death's Door slam in the back of his mind and walked forward.

'Gulnar' in the Turkish tongue means 'flower' but in the secret broken speech of the Welsh Fae it means 'spider'. A spider, as Gulnar had observed many

48

times, sensed its prey through vibrations along its web. Grief was one such vibration; as was pride, and hate, and fear, and greed. Nottingham Castle was always loud with such vibrations and—since the death of Gisburne's mother—the vibrations had got so loud that they now rang in Gulnar's split-mind, until he could no longer resist moving to the centre of the web.

The sorcerer's original intent had been to burrow into the Sherwood and plot his revenge from there, but Herne's protections were too strong; even for him. But there, at the castle, was an opportunity. The grief-stricken lieutenant was wide open.

Gulnar's old master, Owen of Clun, used to attack from the borders when his rivals were weak. A funeral would often set the date for an unexpected assault on longed-for-land, and Owen rose high and fast using such tactics. He was despised of course, but that made little difference to a warrior who wanted power over love. Clun's example was one of the things that made Gulnar who he was. Love needed to be caught, tied up in a sack, and thrown away into a river and forgotten. Everything must be forgotten.

Gisburne, by contrast, wanted both power and love. It was this which made him weak. So, the spider had made his preparations.

Before he'd set out on his current path, he'd taken beetroot wine and mixed it with barleycorn into a paste with nightshade. It was a poison fused with antidote which, when rubbed into the skin, aged and distressed it. The paste was cruel, and the skin would flare and wrinkle but, in time, return to its original state. Gulnar became old. He wore the clothes of a tinker from Stoke.

It hadn't taken long to make the largest of the caves located beneath Nottingham Castle into a hermitage. A dark forgotten place for dark vengeful deeds.

These hollows had little practical value and were no real sanctuary against the weather. They were, however, close enough to make a convenient web that would surely ensnare Gisburne.

His preparations made, Gulnar set himself in a leaky entrance (not far from the courtyard), which Gisburne would often use on his way from the stables and smiled. He could sense the hate and anger leaking from the castle walls; the sheriff and his servant were arguing. Gulnar could not hear their words, but he could feel their emotions.

The vibrations were strong. The fly would be caught soon.

Years of practicing sorcery had told him he

should always listen to his instinct, his inner-eye—
the vibrations. And he did so now… and they told
him that the time was right.

Getting up, Gulnar rolled the stones out in front
of the cave as makeshift seats. He was sure to make
the smoothest and the flattest the one for Sir Guy.
Comfort would not be enough and so he marked
the stone with a glamour. It now looked more
comfortable than it was.

The chamber would be made next. A room
without walls. Around the stones he drew the star
and within the star a triangle and within that a shape
which had no name but was shown to him once in a
dream. These markings were made in the earth and
carved out by his yew staff and named by Gulnar on
the wind. The markings could not be seen but, like
the wind, were very much there.

Once sat with him, the only sounds Gisburne—
his fly—would hear would be that of his voice. For
some that would have been enough, but Gulnar did
not like to leave things to fate. Some worshipped
and trusted Fate but Gulnar knew how capricious
she could be and so layered his enchantments
one atop of another until they were like the
honeycombs of the castle beehives nearby; complete
in themselves but made stronger by each other.

Eventually, satisfied with his work, he waited. He enjoyed waiting. It always made the consumption sweeter.

Gulnar smelt Gisburne before he saw him. The stench of wine reminded him of his father, as did the nobleman's angry childish scowl. Gulnar had surrounded himself in a fog which he kept in his bag. Gisburne was staring straight at him but could not see the sorcerer. The obfuscation wasn't strictly necessary, but Gulnar liked to make an entrance and fancied that a sudden appearance would imprint himself more fully on the fly's mind.

'Funny how we look but don't see, isn't it, young man?' Gulnar said, appearing from his invisible mist.

A sword flew from a sheath and into a firm grip. Gisburne was fast but, on seeing the old hermit in front of him, clearly felt no threat and so returned the sword to his belt. It didn't hurt that Gulnar had scented the area with lemon balm. How peaceful this place was...

No need for violence.

'Fine instinct you have there. I can see you are a soldier of calibre.' Grunting, Gisburne returned his sword to his belt. 'I'm glad someone thinks so.'

'Oh?' The tinker's hat Gulnar wore slipped forward over his face. 'You are unappreciated?'

'You have no idea!'

'Then tell me, young man.' Gulnar spoke in a compassionate, soothing way—as one might to a cat when you wanted it sat in your lap. He patted the rock next to him. 'Take the weight off your boots.'

Gisburne made some demands, 'Who are you?' 'Why are you here..?' But the sorcerer was barely listening.

Allowing his tongue to respond, he disconnected his mind and communed with the wind again; Gulnar was incanting.

But then a thought distracted him. *Gisburne's hair.* Locks like a wheat-field. Locks. Loxley. Huntington. *How like his hair was to Huntington's. Could they be..?*

Gisburne caught Gulnar's stare and began to rise quizzically.

He should not have let his concentration slip. 'What happened to your hair?'

'The sheriff threw a goblet of wine at me,' pouted the fly.

'He never did!' He muttered, 'what a cruel thing to do.'

How like a child he was, thought Gulnar. *Perhaps, there was no need for magic after all?*

Gulnar simpered and sympathized as Gisburne moaned, sharing his plans of escape, of a return to a past he'd live in Gloucester. And as he listened, the sorcerer sowed doubts in the fly's simple mind. He had learned such things at court. Manipulation. It was what ordinary humans did instead of magic. A different kind of spell casting and so many of them were well practiced at it.

They talked some more.

Gisburne was captivated as Gulnar questioned his desire to leave. 'Are you sure?' he asked, 'The Duke of Gloucester might prefer you to stay. He might need you to be *here*. In a position to influence… events.'

'Events?' Guy's eyes narrowed in suspicion. You know the Duke of Gloucester?'

'Of him, certainly.'

'How could the likes of you know…'

The Sorcerer crossed and uncrossed his legs. 'You should not underestimate anyone, Sir Guy. The man you see before you now is not the man I once was.' Gulnar spoke in his hermit's voice. He enjoyed telling the truth, especially when it was wrapped within a lie.

Gisburne was still talking, but Gulnar no longer listened. His mouth spoke the words that his fly wanted to hear. Suggestions that the sheriff was cruel, corrupt… insane? No, not insane, just cruel. These suggestions kept the deputy hooked upon his words. Gulnar knew he could devour him now— make him his forever—but, no, not yet. Not until he served his purpose.

A thoughtful silence came over the fly, before he said, 'I should go now.'

'No, you shouldn't. Not yet.'

'But…'

'Your hair is sticky, a bruise is forming on your face, and your uniform is stained with dots of wine.'

The deputy hesitated, his hand coming to his hair. *That golden hair again.* 'I'll have to go back into the castle and change. I suppose I ought to pack up my belongings before I go.'

Gulnar dropped his hermit voice and spoke in his own. In that moment, the illusion no longer mattered. 'Later.'

'If I want to leave now, then I…'

Gulnar needed to keep things secure. Incantation upon incantation upon incantation. He held up his hand, upon which was drawn a mesmeric symbol. Gisburne was compelled by it, transfixed by it, although his eyes would have no memory of it at all. The hand and the symbol held him as Gulnar returned to his use of the hermit voice.

'Forgive me, Sir, I forget myself. I merely thought that you may wish to stay a little longer. Give yourself time to calm down and think of a proper plan. After all, you don't know where you are going, do you?'

The unseeable symbol had drifted from his hand and, like a parasite, snaked into Gisburne's mind. It began to eat his memory and increase his uncertainty.

'Glous...'

Gulnar shook his head, a small smile forming on his thin lips. Gisburne found himself saying. 'No... not Gloucester... I decided I didn't want to go there.'

'That's right. You thought going there was a bad idea.'

'I did. I forgot.' Gisburne ran a hand over his face, trying to wipe the fog from his brain. 'Who are you? Did you say, I...'

Gulnar produced his staff, made from the yew of an ancient sacrificial altar. Over the centuries, more blood had been spilled on that yew than in the whole of the crusades. It was said that it was so soaked in death that, should Death's Door need to be kept open, this staff might well do the job. Gisburne was looking blankly at the staff and its master, waiting to be told what to do.

Gulnar moved towards the cave. 'Why not come inside? You can wash, and I'll tell you my story...'

The fire in his cave was blood-red, and the logs imbued with the sickly-smelling plant were keeping him as pliant as willow.

In the crimson light, Gisburne looked even more and more like Robert of Huntingdon. Gulnar's blood rose and he found himself reaching for his yew staff, ready to beat his enemy. The hooded man without a head. The hooded man crushed in a cave. Herne's son broken and returned to soil. A crackle from the fire snapped Gulnar from his delusion. He rallied himself. Magic was like the fire itself; a useful tool but, if you weren't careful, it would turn

against its user in a heartbeat, in a second, in a…
spell.

Gisburne spoke slowly. 'How long have you
been here?' he asked, as he examined the web that
he had no idea he was trapped in.

'Somewhere between a day and forever.'

Gisburne's hand came to his head, cradling it as
if it ached, and a yawn escaped his lips.

'You are tired, Sir Guy. Please rest whilst I heat
some water for you to wash in.'

'I'm fine.'

'Are you?' Gulnar shrewdly asked the soldier, his
mind tightening the incantations while he spoke
foreign words of kindness.

'A headache, that's all.'

'Really? Is that all? Don't you feel as if you've been
awake for somewhere between today and forever?'

Gulnar had to concentrate on not letting out a
cough of snide laughter as Gisburne tore his gaze
from the intoxicating flames.

'You said that before.'

'Yes.'

Gisburne blinked before finding his eyes forced
by an invisible force back to the fire. 'The flames are
red.'

'Yes.'

'But… they're usually orange… aren't they?'

'And how often do you look at something as mundane as a fire, Sir Guy? Isn't that a task you leave to the castle's servants?'

'Well, I…'

'You look a little unwell. Rest a while.' As the fly sat, the spider poured him a tankard. 'Here. The sheriff's finest claret. Better to drink it than to wear it.'

Gulnar let his mouth free, answering his prisoner's inane queries as he continued with the real work—the important work. Revenge. He only phased back into the conversation as Gisburne's words faltered, dripping uncertainty.

'And you… who are you again?'

'Someone who has lived here for somewhere between today and forever.'

'You said…'

'That before? Yes. Three times in fact.' Gulnar crouched, his legs frog-like, his back ramrod-straight. 'A powerful number, three, don't you think? It's usually sufficient to do the trick, although, occasionally, reminders are required.'

'Reminders..?'

Cutting in, the old man stretched out a hand and grabbed his staff, holding it tightly as he said,

'Three can be lucky. It *will* be lucky for me—but to make sure of that luck… to ensure that I won't fail this time, I need to practice.'

'Practice?' Gisburne swayed slightly and blinked, as if struggling to focus.

'Practice, yes. I've tried twice before you see, and both times…' Gulnar paused, then continued, 'It does not matter… I will *not* fail again. *He* will not beat me.'

'Who won't beat you? Who *are* you?' Gisburne said.

The fly was coming to his senses.

Gulnar felt an edge of panic as the man turned to leave. He didn't like the sensation—*he* was the one who should be in control. The spider controlled the fly.

The sorcerer reached for the wine. 'No, you must stay. You need to rest, my Lord. Remember?'

Emergency measures of 'unholy water' were called for. The claret was warming in the cauldron that was hung over the fire. It was drugged, of course—another magic practiced by those without the craft. Still, Gulnar was not above using such methods.

'I need to rest.' A puzzled expression crossed Gisburne's face as the hermit passed him a fresh cup.

Gulnar watched as Gisburne drank greedily. Some things, however crude, could always be relied upon.

'Nice claret.'

'The sheriff's finest, with a hint of something extra.'

'It is pleasant. Soothing.' Gisburne said, dopily wiping his mouth with his sleeve.

Unseen by his companion, Gulnar opened his other hand. Another fog-scriven incantation was inscribed upon it. He spoke silent words of magic, but all the fly heard were secret dreams of happiness. *It will make you happy. You secretly yearn to be happy. You will help me, and I will help you to fulfil that wish.*

Gisburne's eyes began to bleed tears. It was a sign that the magic was set, and he would have no memory of it. Now, as all things were done, the sorcerer commanded his fly to leave. The fly—staggering under the wine, the drugs, and the enchantment—began to head towards the mouth of the cave.

'You will come back, bringing some herbs and water with you...'

'I will?'

'Yes, you will.'

'What herbs? How many?'

'Trust your instincts, Sir Guy.' The hermit gave a soft chuckle. 'I know which and how many, so you'll know too. Go now.'

A fool once said that the powers of light and darkness needed to be in balance. But surely the light and the dark devoured each other at every opportunity? Gulnar wondered if he might one day have the power to extinguish the sun and then the light would be gone.

Balance was weakness.

Balance was a state that gave permission when it should simply have taken what it wanted. The light gave and Gulnar could not understand why generosity was seen as a virtue when it was, in essence, surrendering something at its own expense. Only the dark understood how to profit, how to exploit, how to gain advantage. It was why he served darkness, why he *was* darkness; because, at the end of the day, there was always night and, at the end of the day, darkness would always win. *He* would always win.

Clay.

Gulnar had planned to fetch clay from the river himself, but he was always uncomfortable around water. To spare him the task, as soon as Gisburne had returned with the herbs, the sorcerer had sent him out twice more. First for clay, and then for water.

There was relief in Gisburne serving him in such a way. Twice he had been taken by the waters to Death's Door. First, as a child, and then after Marion of Leaford had confronted him at Cromm Cruac. Like his father, she attacked him. With his father it was wine and with her it was with water that had been blessed by the God of Light. It had burned him. He still had the scars and there wasn't a spell, ointment, or tincture in the world that was powerful enough to remove them. The light had made its mark on him; he, the thing of darkness. *Was this balance?*

He had sought an answer to the light after he'd left Clun –a means to bring only darkness upon the world– and he'd discovered Fenris. If Fenris was a powerful as some believed, perhaps—after he had put out the sun—he would take Heaven itself and all light would be forever gone. That was a happy thought.

Herne was against him, of course. The antlered idiot who dressed himself as the thing he hunted.

Why become the thing you killed? Not so much Herne the Hunter but Herne the Hunted. And Gulnar had tried to hunt him many times, but Herne drew great strength from the forest. His power was, like the trees of Sherwood, deeply rooted. Gulnar would use his power to destroy the myth of Robin Hood and then destroy the man, Robert of Huntingdon.

When Robin Hood was gone, Herne would struggle to keep darkness from encroaching on his kingdom.

Gulnar had felt it when Loxley had died. Darkness had increased at the expense of the light. Such a thing could happen again. Would happen again. The sorcerer had foreseen a way to strike at Herne's heart and remove his antlered head. He would take those antlers and wear them upside down around his neck when he took God's throne. He believed that now. Believed it because Fenris the Wolf had told him this in person on the night of the last blood moon.

The Wolf had visited him in a nightmare. It came to him as a shape from the North and it scared even the fae who frequently populated his dreams. They scattered at the coming of the wolf. The fact that it struck horror in them appealed to Gulnar. Fear was always a compass for him. It helped point you towards the dark. Allaying himself with a power like that could give him the final victory he so thirsted for. He was a creature of want and Fenris had what he wanted.

In the confines of his dreams, the wolf understood and agreed that the light needed to be put out, but there was a price. There is always a price.

The wolf insisted that Gulnar needed to sire sons. Wild and furious and without mercy. Without light. They would roam as a pack, and they would kill and consume. They would be named the Sons of Fenris. *But how to achieve this...*

Fenris had given him a word and the word was... *Clay.*

Gisburne had finally returned with the herbs and clay, and also—eventually—with some water.

It was many weeks since Cromm Cruac, since the almost-drowning, and since Fenris had come to him and shown him the way forward, the way to extinguish his enemies.

Now, after all the preparations, he would finally make what should not be made.

Gisburne stared blankly ahead as Gulnar got to work shaping the river-clay into an oblong. There was already a problem as the fool had not brought enough of the stuff.

He should have gone to the river himself, but he had been afraid.

Why had I succumbed to the fear instead of using it to point him in the right direction? If I'd have gone myself, then there would be enough.

Gisburne smiled at him, and Gulnar wanted to strike him then and there.

'No,' the wolf in Gulnar's mind said.

No, thought Gulnar. *To get what I want, I must obey.*

The sorcerer, on his knees, continued to work the clay. He muttered the words he had learned from the wolf. The sounds were complicated. They were not English words but more guttural sounds that hurt his throat and chest to speak. He spoke them anyway, just as he had been taught.

A moment later, he became aware of another presence.

Gisburne had returned to the cave. He was watching him work, his eyes wide.

The nobleman put his hands into the clay and the clay overtook them. It became so that the clay, the living moving clay, began to draw the life from the man himself. It was moulding him, and not the other way around. Gulnar could hear the fog in Gisburne's mind as it said: *This is the way… this is how Robin Hood will meet his end. This is it… He'll end when…*

'When the Sons of Fenris cry through the night,' finished Gulnar.

Both men were smiling now, as the clay oozed, increasing in size and shape. Suddenly, Gisburne paused, his face creased in confusion, 'What did you say?'

'I…'

The sorcerer's words died on his lips as both heard voices from without the cave. Gulnar smiled with his many teeth. His wolf teeth. He felt delighted. He could see the intruders in his mind's eye.

Little John and his woman were coming into the web. He had not planned for this, but why would a spider resent more flies?

'We are about to have guests, Sir Guy. Once they come in here, you must keep working while I greet them.' Gulnar said, as he moved towards the shadows by the door. He did not need a fog to hide himself for the dark would be enough.

Gisburne did as he was bidden and began to shape the clay into a resemblance of himself. Although Gulnar knew it was really the other way around. He muttered the words of Fenris faster now, harder now, and with more intent. The clay was beginning to take possession of Gisburne's soul.

From outside, two voices rang out. The man said, 'You go inside, Meg, I'll just make sure no one followed us.' The woman said 'Oh John! It'll be fine. Let's get in the cave. We'll be safe in there.'

Gulnar was, for a moment, distracted and misspoke a word. The fire crackled angrily in response. A warning. He must concentrate. He redoubled his efforts. He must speak faster and keep the words clear or else all would be lost. The clay was becoming unstable and violent.

Little John and Meg came rushing inside far sooner than he had anticipated. They were filled with love and its very presence began to repel the clay

68

from Gisburne's hands. Gulnar had not reckoned with this. Love. Love needed to be caught up, tied up in a sack, and thrown away into a river and forgotten.

Everything must be forgotten.

He was forgetting the words.

They were giggling. But then, in an instant, they stopped.

Gulnar was foggy. Time froze as his magical strength was pulled in different directions—the clay, Gisburne, and now the intruders. He had the strength to cast one last spell. He targeted it at the biggest threat—John Little. He stared at the man—used his eyes, the windows of the soul, to open a door—and began to bore and burrow into the outlaw's mind. But it was not easy, the man had been enchanted before and part of him knew how to resist.

Gulnar, his voice overtaken by Fenris, screamed through his broken throat. 'GRAB THEM!'

Gisburne was propelled then by a force he had never experienced. His body, like a puppet, was wrenched from the clay and—like the clay—he took possession of the woman. Meg struggled and began to scream.

Gulnar's eyes bulged. Hate creased his face. 'GULNAR!' shouted Little John, in shock, which also seemed to shock Gisburne too.

A spell formed on Gulnar's lips—but he was too slow. Little John's cry of recognition dovetailed with his quarterstaff landing on Gulnar's shoulder with a sickening thwack.

The clay seemed to scream and writhe in anger, as the sorcerer's head hit the floor.

Gulnar's vision blurred. Then there was nothing but the coming of an unconsciousness. An unconsciousness that resounded with the howl of a giant wolf's displeasure.

Gisburne was still wrestling with the outlaw's woman when Gulnar awoke, but she was fighting like a cornered wild boar. The period of enforced sleep had clearly been brief, from the glancing blow, but his attacker seemed to have deserted his supposed love.

Casting his personal moment of humiliation aside, Gulnar leapt up to help Gisburne, working swiftly to bind her. He stuffed a filthy rag into Meg's mouth, before pressing her to the floor and into the quietened clay.

As he worked, he glanced at Gisburne. He could see the man beginning to wonder where he'd met this woman before. The enchantment was waning. All spells were sorrowfully short, and this one was already coming to an end. The sorcerer needed to rally his only troop, and he mused aloud as he regarded Meg.

'This is better than I could have hoped. I'd thought she would turn and run and that it would be the bearded giant who assisted us. What more fitting revenge than to use one of Hood's men against him! But she... well, she is so much more... fitting.'

'Why's that?' asked Gibsurne.

'Because you only brought me a small amount of clay.'

Gisburne looked hurt at the accusation. *He's like a child. How does De Rainault put up with him!*

Gulnar swallowed the desire to berate Gisburne. *I can punish him later, when he's of no more use to me... Perhaps this was how it was meant to be...* He paused, before muttering to himself, 'No matter. A smaller figure to copy will help our cause.'

'Cause?' queried Gisburne.

Gulnar hid his exasperation. 'You have heard my name cried out by Little John, and yet you still do not remember me, Sir Guy?'

'Remember...'

'We met, albeit briefly, at Huntingdon Castle. I'm sure, somewhere deep under my enchantment, your mind is telling you what I am.'

'Castle... Candles and a woman... Leaford... Huntingdon... Robert...' Gisburne whispered, 'Owen of Clun.'

'Well done. My master was Owen of Clun.' Gulnar kicked Meg's bound body. 'This creature's lover works for the man who destroyed him. And I will have my revenge. I *will*.'

'But... how... when..?'

It was a wonder, Gulnar thought, that the man had enough brains to put food in his mouth and a fork to his lips.

'Sometime between now and forever.' Gulnar smiled as his words pulled Gisburne back under the enchantment.

Together they worked, sorcerer and soldier, pressing and moulding the bubbling clay. It hissed and fought as it became the very image of Meg of Wickham.

Gulnar laboured hard to forge his mind into the well of clay. Meg's mind. A task made all the harder by the fact that the real Meg was spitting hate behind her gag, and Gisburne would not stop talking.

'I don't understand.'

72

'Because I do not wish you to.' Snapped Gulnar, running his gnarled hands over the length of the clay. 'When you are my son, you will know. And then you will walk willingly at my side with no need for incantations.'

'Your son?'

'There will be many sons, and they will howl to the moon. I have seen it.'

'I…'

Gulnar held up his hand with the invisible sign on it and Gisburne's mouth clamped shut. 'There will be time to explain later. Now, we need to hurry. It won't be long before that giant oaf returns to try and save his wench.'

An indignant squeak from Meg made Gulnar snap out an order, 'Be silent, *both* of you. I need to concentrate.'

Getting back to his task, he worked the clay more carefully in the final stages. Fenris howled instructions in his mind, the first of which was to tell him he needed to finish this task alone.

'Go now, soldier.'

Immersed in his work, it was a few seconds before Gulnar realised his enchanted assistant hadn't been listening.

'I told you to go!' Gulnar jumped to his feet. 'Hurry! Go! For now, your usefulness is over. The sheriff will need you and *you* will need him—I will see you again.'

'But… when will that be?'

'Sometime between now and forever.'

As soon as Gisburne had gone, Gulnar began to pace his cave, stepping over the real Meg of Wickham, who had finally passed out, exhausted on the floor.

Meg of Gulnar, however, was wide awake. Her clay form still unresolved, but gradually forming both in Gulnar's mind and on the cave's floor. She was looking at him, her eyes beginning to focus, and the clay looked increasingly flesh-like.

The creature he'd created was no longer a thing. It was a woman.

She was looking at him as Meg of Wickham looked at John Little.

Love.

Love?

Love needed to be caught up, tied up in a sack, and thrown away into a river and forgotten. That had been the only lesson his father had taught him, and Gulnar embraced it. To think otherwise was to put oneself in harm's way. Love was nothing but an illusion. Beauty, nothing but a charm that would one day be undone by the most powerful spell of all time.

After all, had he not easily charmed the Maid Marion, so that she fell in love with Owen of Clun?

Fall was the right word. To fall in love. Gulnar did not want to fall. He wanted to rise.

Meg of Gulnar was silently reaching out to him.

He continued to feed her with his mind. She would soon be ready. He, with great effort, continued the final incantations with his parched voice. He need not look at her. Not now. Now his practice was over—his experiment a success—a small but perfect human replica oozing with a clay formed potential. A potential for revenge.

Gulnar snarled out a smile. He knew the secret of creation. Fenris had given him the knowledge. If he could raise an army, the Sons of Fenris could take Robert of Huntington.

He could see the future so clearly. He knew what must be done and how to do it.

Robin of Gulnar to fight Robin of Sherwood. A clay slave who would serve the dark with wolf's teeth.

That was what he needed to do. He put his last few items in his bag. Replacing the tinker's hat atop his head to hide his face, he allowed his skin to return to normal now—there was no trace of the old hermit about him, save the clothes that he wore.

Gulnar picked up his knife. He had one last duty to perform before he could flee the cave. He must kill Meg of Wickham and take her body from this place. When his enemies returned, they would find Meg of Gulnar and think her their friend. She would willingly go with them and then cause havoc in their camp. She would whisper to John to betray the others, and he would obey because he loved her.

Meg of Gulnar began to gurgle—struggling to form her first words just as Meg of Wickham began to come back to consciousness.

Wondering what his creations' first utterances would be, Gulnar hurried forwards, raising his knife, aiming it at his prisoner.

Meg of Wickham bit down on the rag that muzzled her, and she screamed with all the breath that was left in her body.

Closing his eyes tightly, muttering his final words of magic, Gulnar threw his arm back, ready to plunge the blade into the real Meg's heart.

So focused was he on his goal, Gulnar did not see a frightened sheriff rush into the cave, with John Little on his heels. Wrapped within the magic he'd been about to cast, the invaders' shouts were deaf to his ears. For the second time, he did not see the oak quarterstaff until it was too late.

As it felled him like a tree, Gulnar felt the screams of Meg of Gulnar echo through his body as the Sheriff of Nottingham broke up the clay; and in that moment, he too screamed. He screamed like he had never screamed before.

And then there was nothing.

Gulnar awoke in the cave to the sound of the Sheriff's men walling him up inside. They had taken his things. Even his clothes. He was left naked and alone.

Almost alone.

She was still there. Fragments of her. Clay pieces of her all around him. His greatest incantation—

along with its burgeoning voice—had been destroyed.

The light went out when the final stone was put in place, sealing the cave like a tomb.

He was in the dark.

Hours passed.

Shuffling around the empty space, he was surprised to find his yew staff; propped in the corner with an old broom and a forgotten pail. His thin hand wrapped itself around the stave. Although he barely had any strength left, he gripped it fast.

You are going to die.

Gulnar's weary eyes blinked, but he knew better than to ignore the words that blazed across the forefront of his mind.

You must act now. You must remember…

He squeezed his eyes shut, and the staff even tighter, and listened.

You are going to die. You are trapped in a cave, and you are going to die. Unless you remember…

The sorcerer's smooth forehead furrowed. 'Remember… Remember what?'

Opening his eyes, he squinted through the dark, staring at the yew staff in his hand.

The story?

A slow smile crept across his face.

There was the story, of course there was. The story he'd learned as a child. He stared at the yew staff, and felt it pulse in his hand.

It was said that this yew stave was so soaked in death that, should Death's Door need to be kept open, it would serve him well and do that job.

Gulnar closed his eyes again and concentrated.

In the dark of his mind the door came... he didn't hesitate.

Wedging it open with the yew, he ensured it would not shut on him—it would *never* shut on him.

He passed through the doorway as easily as the breeze.

And as he moved, he vowed he would return as fierce as fire.

And then there would be clay—more clay. Better. More powerful.

Gulnar smiled.

He had found a way out. For, as he had known since childhood, Death is always a doorway.

3: GISBURNE

By Jennifer Ash

'Are you with me, Gisburne?'

'Yes, my Lord. Of course.'

'Well it doesn't look like it.' Robert de Rainault, Sheriff of Nottingham, slammed his goblet of wine down so hard that a fountain of claret sloshed across the table. 'In fact, if you'd been more "with me" you might not have made such an unholy mess of the last few days.'

Biting the inside of his lips, Gisburne took a slow deep breath. Long experience told him there was no point in arguing with the sheriff when he was in the mood to enjoy picking holes in his household.

I could have escaped. I had the cross in my hands! If I'd abandoned the hunt for the outlaws, I could have gone away, sold the cross and then I'd have been free.

I blame my mother, if she hadn't shown up then I'd have been thinking more clearly.

A volley of tepid red wine hit Gisburne in the face. Instinct made him jump back and draw his sword at the same time.

'How dare you wave a sword at me?'

Spluttering, anger burning in this throat, Gisburne wiped a hand across his face. Droplets of red wine hung across his blond fringe, dripping down his uniform.

'And how dare you throw wine at me!'

'I will do what I like, Gisburne! You are my servant. My vassal. You are nothing!'

'No! I'm your punchbag! And I'm sick of it!' Gisburne waved his sword under the sheriff's nose, taking a seconds pleasure from the uncertain look in his eye, before he mastered his temptation to run his superior through and sheathed his sword.

Not quite managing to hide a sharp gasp of relief, De Rainault shouted, 'If you are so sick of it, why did you come back? I know you said you'd planned to steal the Cross of St Ciricus for me, but you weren't going to do that, *were* you Gisburne?. You wanted it for yourself.'

Shaking some wine from his hair, Gisburne fixed the sheriff with a glare that would have withered anyone else. 'I did no such thing, but if I had, could you blame me? You treat me like a serf. Everything I do is on your orders, *your* ideas—but when they go wrong—as they *always* do, it's my fault!' Pausing for breath, he lowered his voice, 'Perhaps I would have taken the cross for myself. I don't know. All I do know is that if I hadn't been distracted by the death of my mother, then I'd have succeeded in stealing it and killed that blasted wolfshead—or at least one of his men—in the process.'

'You hated your mother so don't go blaming her demise! When you crawled back here after your latest failure, you were gloating that she was finally gone to join your father in hell. You used to bleat endlessly about them.'

'I did no such thing! And yes, I hated them, but hate is still distracting. Look how damn distracted you are by Robin Hood! Distracted to the point of obsession!'

The slap that landed on Gisburne's cheek left a livid mark almost as red as the wine that had come before it.

For a split second every servant and guard stilled in shock, as if drawing their collective breath. Then, understanding the consequences of having been seen to have witnessed the sheriff assaulting his deputy, the servants hurried about their business with extra speed and the guards pushed their shoulders further back as they stood to attention.

As the hall around him burst back into movement, Guy's hand came to his cheek. He rubbed it slowly, his eyes fixed on the sheriff, hate shining in his eyes. Shocked and humiliated to have been treated so in public, he opened his mouth to speak but no words would come.

Ignoring his deputy's stupefied expression, De Rainault looked away, clicking his fingers for a maid to attend him. 'I'm out of wine.'

As the maid hurried off with the empty flagon, the sheriff turned back to his stunned companion and gave a slow snakelike smile. 'What is it, Gisburne? Finally run out of complaints?'

'You hit me.'

'That's encouraging. I wondered if you'd noticed for a minute there. You aren't the most observant. If you were, then Hood and his men would…'

'No!'

The sharp ferocity of the shout echoed around the hall. This time the stunned silence lasted longer. No one moved.

Gisburne shook. His whole being tightened. Every muscle tense, he glared at his master, rage overtaking him. When the words eventually came, they were little more than a slow mutter.

'I have had enough. I've told you before, I am not your whipping boy.'

'Oh, but you are, Gisburne. You're the best whipping boy there is. You make yourself such an easy target.' The sheriff broke into a cruel chuckle. 'It's only because I enjoy baiting you so much that I've not replaced you! God knows, the Captain of the Guard would do a better job.'

Overwhelmed with betrayal and a nagging sense of his own failure, Gisburne suddenly felt like the little boy who'd never failed to disappoint his parents—unable to meet the exacting standards of a brutal father, or comprehend while his mother did nothing to protect him.

'You are so like my father.'

A frown wiped away the sheriff's gloating smile as the bitterness of Gisburne's words hit him. 'Edmund of Gisburne was a monster.'

'He was. But you are worse.' Breathing heavily, Gisburne glared into the sheriff's gimlet eyes for a few seconds, before he abruptly spun around on the balls of his boots and marched from the hall without a backwards glance.

Guy of Gisburne gripped the handle of his sword as he strode through the castle. He moved blindly, his face and hair sticky from the wine. His cheeks were bright red—as much from embarrassment as the sting of his struck cheek. His head down, his pace fast, he had no idea where he was going. All that mattered was putting some space between himself and the sheriff before he did something that he might not regret, but would certainly take him on a one-way trip to the hangman's noose.

He passed though the corridor to the kitchen without noticing the cloying aroma of spices and rotting meat, and pushed open the large double doors that lead out into the castle's garden.

I'm sick of this life. I have to leave. Here I'm never going to be happy. He gave a derisive snort. *Happy? When was I ever happy!*

Bathed in sunshine, the fresh, summer air was wasted on Gisburne as, his hand on his sheathed sword's handle, he passed the long-neglected beehives, once kept so lovingly by the Lady Marion. Ducking under an unkempt tangle of brambles and low-hanging trees, he reached a wall of rock on the edge of the castle's territory.

Breathing deeply, Gisburne let go of his sword and flexed his hand before looking at his palm. The outline of the handle was visible in his skin from where he'd been gripping the weapon so hard. Staring at the damp wall before him, he leant forward, placing both his palms against the stone, letting its coolness soothe his flesh as he struggled to calm his racing pulse.

It took a few minutes before the birdsong overhead broke through his thoughts. Gisburne looked around him, fully taking in his surroundings for the first time.

The wall against which he rested was sheer. It rose up through the trees to either side of it, like a cliff-face. The stone of the castle wall merged into the natural stone, reminding Gisburne just how well his Norman ancestors had thought out the positioning of the castle. To his left, he assumed an area of woodland he'd never visited ran down to the river. To his right, a tangle of tall, dense foliage smothered what looked like a small hovel.

Curious, Gisburne moved to the right. A moment later, he realised he wasn't looking at an abandoned manmade dwelling or workshop, but a cave; one of the many he knew to be part of Nottingham's ancient past.

'Funny how we look but don't see, isn't it, young man?'

Gisburne had drawn his sword even before he'd fully swung around to see the figure addressing him.

'Fine instinct you have there.' The old man nodded in approval. 'I can see you are a soldier of calibre.'

Grunting, Gisburne returned his sword to his belt. 'I'm glad someone thinks so.'

'Oh?' Tilting his head to one side, this action made the wide-brimmed, badly-fitting, felt hat he wore slip further over his face. 'You are unappreciated?'

'You have no idea!' Gisburne checked over his shoulder, half expecting some of the castle's men-at-arms to come and drag him back to the hall.

'Then tell me, young man.' He patted the rock next to him, 'Take the weight off your boots.'

Guy took one step towards the stranger and then stopped. 'Who are you? What are you doing here?'

'I live here.'

'Live... Does the sheriff know you're here?'

The old man gave him a toothy smile, 'Why would the likes of the sheriff notice a mere hermit?'

Snorting, Gisburne could not argue with the logic as he sat on the proffered rock. 'He barely notices me. Unless he wants to taunt me.'

'Why should he taunt you?'

'He enjoys it. But I've had enough.' Gisburne ran his hands through his hair. 'That's the last time he humiliates me in front of the servants,'

The old man looked at the sorrowful soldier next to him. 'What happened to your hair?'

'The sheriff threw a goblet of wine at me.'

'He never did!' He muttered, 'what a cruel thing to do.'

'De Rainault is a cruel man.' Gisburne snorted. 'That's why I'm leaving.'

'Where will you go?'

'Gloucester.' Guy sat up a little straighter. 'I was page to the duke once. He didn't want me to leave to work for the sheriff. He'll welcome me back and treat me with respect.'

'Umm.' The old man stared forward, his small round eyes sparkling with a youth that belied his wizened face. 'Are you sure? The Duke of Gloucester might prefer you to stay. He might need you to be here. In a position to influence...events.'

'Events?' Guy's eyes narrowed in suspicion. 'You know the Duke of Gloucester?'

'Of him, certainly.'

'How could the likes of you know…'

Brushing his gnarled, pale hands down his tattered cloak, the old hermit crossed and uncrossed his long, spindly legs as he stretched them out before him. 'You should not underestimate anyone, Sir Guy. The man you see before you now is not the man I once was.'

Intrigued, Gisburne asked, 'You once had influence?'

'Let's just say I was well placed to see things. I was trusted to read reactions, make the best of events—guide others with power.'

'And now you are here.' Guy fought back the desire to shudder.

'You would do well to take heed of my reduced circumstances. I was not always a man alone, forced to eke out an existence in a hole in a forgotten part of a madman's castle.'

Gisburne's eyes widened. 'You think the sheriff is mad?'

'Don't you?'

'Angry, yes. Impulsive…impetuous… mean…' Gisburne found himself warming to the theme. 'Petty-minded, greedy, cruel…'

'And insane?'

Staring out across the edge of the forgotten garden towards the sheer wall, Gisburne thought before he answered, an image of De Rainault in his mind. 'Insane… no… not insane. Corrupt and cruel… but not mad.'

The old man chuckled. 'You make that sound like a compliment.'

Gisburne shrugged, 'To him, it probably would be.'

Gisburne felt increasingly uneasy, as he watched the old man from the corner of his eye. *If I leave Nottingham, will I end up like him?* Not wanting to see any correlation between himself and his companion, he said, 'I should go.'

'No, you shouldn't. Not yet.'

'But…'

'Your hair is sticky, a bruise is forming on your face, and your uniform is stained with dots of wine.'

Gisburne groaned, as he brushed pointlessly at a spatter of wine that decorated his livery. 'I'll have to go back into the castle and change.' He hesitated, less sure of his plans to leave than he had been. 'I suppose I ought to pack up my belongings before I go.'

'Later.'

The tone of the hermit's voice was so firm that Gisburne felt himself bristle. 'If I want to leave now, then I…'

The old man held up a placating hand, 'Forgive me, Sir, I forget myself. I merely thought that you may wish to stay a little longer. Give yourself time to calm down and think of a proper plan. After all, you don't know where you are going, do you?'

'Glouc…'

The hermit shook his head, a small smile forming on his thin lips.

Gisburne found himself saying. 'No… not Gloucester… I decided I didn't want to go there.'

'That's right. You thought going there was a bad idea.'

'I did. I forgot.' Gisburne ran a hand over his face. 'Who are you? Did you say I…'

The hermit gripped the end of a long, wooden staff that Gisburne hadn't noticed before. 'Why not come inside? You can wash, and I'll tell you my story.'

'Well, I…'

'Better than facing your future with sticky skin and matted hair.'

'You're right.' Gisburne jumped up, an unfamiliar smile forming on his lips.

Unfolding his bony frame within the billows of his cloak, the old man pointed towards the cave's mouth with the end of his staff. 'Then walk this way.'

The acrid aroma hit Gisburne the second he ducked through the low entrance way. Almost choking as the scent hit the back of his throat, he coughed, his eyes blinking in the half light. A low fire, in the centre of the almost circular space, crackled and hissed beneath a cooking cauldron which had been suspended from chains that, in turn, had been attached to the stone ceiling above. An eclectic assortment of rugs and cloaks hung against the walls, giving an illusion of warmth, but with an underlying suggestion of confinement.

Pausing mid stride, Gisburne felt pinpricks of sweat break out on the back of his neck. Wiping them away, he found his eyes drawn to the dancing flames of the fire. He was faintly aware of a voice at the back of his mind telling him something wasn't right. *But I need to get clean…* Peering around the semi-gloom, his eyes adjusting to the smoky atmosphere, Gisburne was amazed to see wooden shelves around the circumference of the cave; each one full to bursting with jars, bottles, and objects of all sorts, shapes, and sizes.

'How long have you been here?'

'Somewhere between a day and forever.'

Gisburne's head instantly thudded with an ache that made him groan. His vision swam for a split second, as the sickly scent that emanated from the fire made him feel lethargic. A yawn escaped his lips.

'You are tired, Sir Guy.' The old man gestured to a barrel that had been cut in half to form a seat. 'Please rest, while I heat some water for you to wash in.'

'I'm fine.'

'Are you?' The hermit twisted his neck around, peering shrewdly at the soldier.

'A headache, that's all.'

'Really? Is that all?' The hermit gave him an enquiring smile. 'Don't you feel as if you've been awake for somewhere between today and forever?'

Gisburne's gaze rose from where he'd been staring into the flames. 'Didn't you just say that before?'

'Yes.' The hermit laid a fresh log onto the fire. In doing so it changed; the orange flames morphing into a deep, red glow.

Gisburne closed his eyes for a second and opened them again. 'The flames are red.'

'Yes.'

'But...they're usually orange... aren't they?'

'And how often do you look at something as mundane as a fire, Sir Guy? Isn't that a task you leave to the castle's servants?'

'Well, I...'

'You look a little unwell. Rest a while.'

Sitting as bidden, Gisburne watched as his host poured some wine from a jug and passed him a tankard. 'Here. The sheriff's finest claret. Better to drink it than to wear it.'

'How did you get it?'

'A few servants in the castle help me.'

'Oh.' Gisburne massaged his temples. He was sure there was something he was going to do... 'How did you know my name? I didn't tell you who I was.'

'You are an important person here. Of course I know who you are.'

'And you... who are you again?'

'Someone who has lived here for somewhere between today and forever.'

A crease formed on Guy's forehead as he took a sip of the claret. 'You said...'

'…I said that before? Yes. Three times in fact.' The old man sat on a rug next to the fire, his thin legs crossed, his back ramrod straight. 'A powerful number, three, don't you think? It's usually sufficient to do the trick, although, occasionally, reminders are required…'

'Reminders…?'

Cutting in, the old man stretched out a hand and grabbed his staff, holding it tightly as he said, 'Three can be lucky. It *will* be lucky for me—but to make sure of that luck… to ensure that I won't fail this time, I need to practice.'

'Practice?' Gisburne mumbled. The word felt heavy on his lips, as the world around him blurred, and he found himself struggling to focus on the man before him.

'Practice, yes. I've tried twice before you see, and both times…' He broke off as a cruel hardness replaced the smile that had previous shone in his eyes. 'It does not matter… I will *not* fail again. *He* will not beat me.'

'Who won't beat you? Who *are* you?' The sixth sense that had been trying to scream at Gisburne that he needed to get out of there, finally broke through the fog that had been seeping into his mind since he'd walked into the castle garden. He stood up quickly, the abrupt motion creating a draught that sent the cauldron swinging in its chains.

With a speed that belied his age, the hermit leapt up, holding his staff out in front of him. 'No, you must stay. You need to rest, my Lord. Remember?'

'I need to rest.' A puzzled expression on his face, Gisburne sank back onto his seat and drank some more wine. 'Nice claret.'

'The sheriff's finest, with a hint of something extra.'

'It…' Gisburne swallowed some more of the smooth liquid. 'It is pleasant. Soothing.'

'Good. It will make you happy. You secretly yearn to be happy. You will help me, and I will help you to fulfil that wish.' The old man stared into the flames for a while, occasionally glancing up at his guest from beneath the brim of his hat. When Gisburne lowered his tankard to the ground, he gave a slow smile. 'You enjoyed that, Sir Guy?'

'What? Yes… it was lovely.'

'I'm glad.' The old man abruptly jumped to his feet. 'You must go now.'

'Go?'

'Back to the castle. Back to the sheriff. You feel better now, and you'll be very happy to work as De Rainault's deputy, won't you?'

'Yes… yes. Of course.'

'It's your duty.'

'My duty.' A smile creased Gisburne's face. 'Yes. My happy duty.'

'Go, there is much to do before our guests come.'

'Guests?'

'That is correct.'

Guy stood, his legs a fraction unsteady, as he made for the mouth of the cave.

'You will come back, bringing some herbs and water with you.'

'I will?'

'Yes, you will.'

'What herbs? How many?'

'Trust your instincts, Sir Guy.' The hermit gave a soft chuckle. 'I know which and how many, so you'll know too. Go now.'

Pushing open the door to the great hall, an unaccustomed air of wellbeing flowed through Gisburne. He felt light, and free of doubt. Reaching a hand to his face, he felt around his mouth, puzzled to find his lips lifting into a smile.

It was only when his fingertips reached a sticky patch on his cheek that a shadow floated across his mind. *Wasn't I going to have a wash?*

The thought evaporated as he moved through the hall. He had almost reached the corridor that led to the kitchen, when he was vaguely aware of a sound. *A shout. Someone's shouting at me.*

'Gisburne! Where the *hell* have you been?'

Turning in the direction of the hectoring voice, Gisburne's grin widened. 'My Lord! How nice to see you.'

'What?'

'I said, it was nice to…'

'I heard you, Gisburne. What is the matter with you?' The sheriff got off his chair and moved closer to his deputy.

'Nothing, my Lord.'

'Why are you smiling?'

'I'm happy, my Lord.'

'Happy?' De Rainault's eyes narrowed at the unfamiliar concept. 'And when did you develop this taste for luxuries?'

'My Lord?'

'Oh, never mind. Go and change your uniform, for goodness sake. You're covered in wine and smell like a bonfire.'

Bonfire… there was a red fire… red… Where? His smile dipped for a split second as his mind battled with itself. *Where was the fire?… When…? Somewhere between today and forever.*

'Gisburne!' The sheriff's voice cut through his thoughts.

'My Lord?'

'Go and wash. You're a mess.'

'Yes, my Lord. Certainly.'

Gisburne gave a low bow and glided off towards his quarters. *What a nice man.*

Gisburne hadn't been able to understand the bewilderment of the servants as he'd wandered around the kitchen looking for herbs. They'd backed away from him, and yet were still helpful. In fact, they helped him with extreme speed.

When he'd thanked a young maid for giving him the herbs he wanted…. *What herbs were they again..?* she'd been terrified.

I must be nicer to the servants. They are so helpful.

Placing his collection of herbs into a cloth bag, Gisburne strode back to the hall, picking up a flagon of his wine as he approached the sheriff. 'Would you like some claret, my Lord?'

'Yes.' The sheriff's eyes narrowed, as he held out his goblet. 'Are you feeling quite well, Gisburne?'

'Never better, my Lord.'

'And you haven't had any sort of accident? A knock on the head, perhaps?'

'No, my Lord, I'm very well, thank you.'

'Then, for goodness sake, sit down and wipe that grin off your face, it's unsettling me.' The sheriff pointed to the chair opposite him. 'I want to talk to you about Robin Hood. It's high time that…'

'I'm terribly sorry, my Lord, but I can't join you now.'

'Can't?'

'There's someone I need to help. A little old man.'

The fine spray of wine that shot from the surprised sheriff's lips narrowly missed Gisburne's fresh uniform. 'Help someone? You?'

'Yes, my Lord.' Gisburne topped up the sheriff's goblet, 'so, if you'll excuse me, I really must go.'

Oblivious to the tirade of disapproval that followed him as he left the hall, Gisburne's grin widened with each step he took closer to the rear of Nottingham castle and the cave.

Helping someone felt good. It was such an unaccustomed sensation, that he paused in his stride to savour the moment. Unhooking the cloth bag from his belt, he stared at it. *Did he tell me why he wanted these herbs?* Dismissing the question as unimportant, he moved forward.

Stooping through the mouth of the cave, the sickly aroma of the enclosed space went unnoticed as he saw the old man hunched over the cauldron. He was muttering something under his breath that Gisburne couldn't quite hear.

Opening his mouth to announce his arrival, Gisburne found there was no need, for the man had already swivelled around to face him. A long, bony arm had reached out and snatched the bag of herbs. 'And the water?'

'I'll fetch it now.' A trickle of uncertainty ran through Gisburne's body, as he stared at the gnarled man.

'Go quickly. We have much to do. I need a barrel full. The water must be clean.'

'Clean.'

'Get it now.'

'Now?'

'Go now, Sir Guy.' The old man's voice took on a hissing rasp. 'Now—not sometime between now and forever—NOW.'

'Yes. I'll go now.'

The hermit turned back to the cauldron, dropping the herbs in one at a time, as he added, 'And then I need clay. Lots and lots of clay.'

The castle's kitchen staff had jumped into action. The water had been pumped from the well, and a barrel had been filled and prepared for Gisburne with a speed that, the sheriff's deputy suspected, came more from a desire to remove him from the kitchen than to obey his orders.

As he rolled the barrel across the castle gardens, he didn't have time to think about the staff's reaction. He had another worry. *Clay… where will I get clay?*

An image flashed through his mind—an unwanted memory of a personal encounter with the sticky clay that lined the banks of some portions of the river. He cringed as he recalled falling into clinging clay and mud as he fought Robin Hood! The smile on Gisburne's face disappeared and a fury raced through him that was so strong, it made him stagger.

Reaching out, steadying himself on the top of the side of the barrel, his body shook as he clearly saw a vision of his own body being dragged through the clay by the wolfshead's hands, his chainmail weighing him down further. The sound of squelchy, wet mud hindering his movements, whilst vicious punches were connecting with his bruised body, resounded through Gisburne. His memory relived the experience of being unable to stop the dowery being stolen, from a wedding no one wanted to take place; humiliating him—again—in front of his master.

The hermit's voice echoed around the cave and into Gisburne's thoughts. 'That's what he does, Sir Guy. Herne's Son lives to humiliate us. It will never matter what face he wears; he will always seek to destroy you and I.'

As the vision of his past failure faded, Gisburne saw the truth of the old man's words. *I must get that clay… the clay will help. Herne's Son will be defeated by…clay?* He paused; feeling sure he must have got that wrong. It seemed so ridiculous. And yet…

Staring blankly at the barrel, Gisburne frowned. 'What am I doing?' He turned back to castle, intending to yell out an order for some servants to come and take the barrel to wherever it needed to go, when the sight of the cave reminded him how important it was to be helpful. *An old man needs some water, and I must be kind. I will take him the barrel and then I will go to the river and get some clay.*

Gisburne's muddled mind didn't give him the chance to wonder how the hermit had managed to cut into his private thoughts when he wasn't even there.

'You're smiling again, Gisburne.'

'Yes, my Lord.'

As he sat down to a plate of roast pork and chicken, Gisburne felt the lips at the corner of his mouth twitch, as if they were trying to fall into their familiar scowl but the muscles wouldn't oblige.

The sheriff stabbed a chicken leg with his dagger. 'What's this I hear about you requesting a barrel of water?'

'Is that a problem, my Lord?'

The sheriff gave his deputy a hard stare. 'What are you up to, Gisburne?'

'I've been with an old…' Leaning forwards, Gisburne felt a suffocating wave of sickly-scented nausea rise in him. His head spun with dizziness. The sound of the sheriff shouting for the steward felt as if it was coming from a long way away, as he crashed heavily onto a chair. Gisburne scrubbed at his throat, as a rasping voice whispered at the back of his mind.

You are my deputy now. The sheriff does not deserve to know.

Spluttering, Gisburne mumbled, 'He doesn't deserve to know.'

'Who doesn't deserve to know what?'

Aware of his superior staring at him, Gisburne's previous lightness washed back over him. Sitting up straight, all signs of his choking fit gone, he smiled serenely at the sheriff. 'Would you like some claret, my Lord?'

An angry fist came down hard against the table. 'What I'd like, Gisburne, is an explanation.'

'About what, my Lord?'

'You keep smiling! It's unnerving me.'

Offended, Gisburne stood up, 'I'm not going to apologise for experiencing a sense of peace, my Lord.'

'Experiencing a sense of peace?! You incredulous cretin!' The sheriff's eyes bulged. 'That's it! You're clearly ill. Go to your quarters, Gisburne. Go and sleep off whatever it is you've drunk that has made you so...so...'

'So what, my Lord?'

'So disgustingly cheerful!' De Rainault's bewildered anger turned to frustrated curiosity as he noted the soiled hem of his deputy's cloak, 'and what the hell is that mud doing on your uniform?'

Gisburne swept from the great hall with a nagging feeling that his new friend wasn't going to be pleased with him. The trouble was, he couldn't work out why.

'I've done all he asked, I've been kind, helpful. He didn't even blanch at the clay's stagnant stench.'

Dismissing the now familiar suspicion of something not being quite right, that trickled down his spine as simply him being tired and fed up with the sheriff's regular treatment, Gisburne wove his way through the narrow stone corridors towards the gardens.

Once he was within sight of the cave, the air of lightness returned, along with his smile. *He won't be cross with me. He's not the sheriff. I'm helping him.*

Everything that had previously sat upon the caves' cluttered floor, apart from the fire, had been moved. The hermit was on his knees, muttering something unintelligible over a mass of clay that he was kneading into a huge, oblong shape.

Gisburne hovered uncertainly on the threshold for a second, but then found himself propelled towards the sticky, grey mass.

'You already know what to do.' The hermit whispered. 'You've always known; sometime between now and forever.'

Dropping to his knees, Gisburne plunged his hands into the watery clay mix and found he really did know what to do—he had always known… *This is the way… this is how Robin Hood will meet his end. This is it…He'll end when…*

'When the Sons of Fenris cry through the night.'

Gisburne froze as his companion's words broke into his thoughts for a second time, their certainty reverberating through the cave, making the fire gutter and the air chill around them. 'What did you say?'

'I…'

The sound of movement outside the cave made both men stop what they were doing and turn to the entrance.

Gisburne felt panicked, but one glance at the hermit calmed him. He was looking delighted. 'We are about to have guests, Sir Guy. Once they come in here, you must keep working while I greet them.'

'They might not come in.'

'They'll come.' The old man smiled. 'You'll be glad to see old… friends, I'm sure.'

Gisburne continued to work. Only now did he register what his hands had been doing. He wasn't just kneading the clay: he was moulding it. Forming it. Shaping it.

The sound of footsteps outside was now accompanied by two hushed voices, both low and cut with laughter. As the newcomer's voices became louder, closer, Guy found his arms and hands moving faster, squeezing and pressing the clay.

How do I know what to do? A thick sweat broke out on Gisburne's forehead. *Why am I here? Who is this man who…?*

The sound of a female voice broke through his anxiety. Soft, firm…determined.

'There it is, John! Told you! Come on.'

I know that voice… I know it… Small… serf…

'You were right, lass.'

A second voice joined the first. Male. Surprised. Cautious. More familiar… A prickle of fear ran through Gisburne as, with each new sound from the figures outside of the cave, the hermit muttered faster; his words making the clay before them change shape more quickly under their combined touch.

'You go inside, Meg, I'll just make sure no one followed us.'

'Oh, John! It'll be fine. Let's get in the cave. We'll be safe in there.'

Guy froze. The cave was suddenly incredibly hot as the fire's red flames shot upwards. The man next to him was whispering faster and faster. The clay before him was changing, moving as if of its own volition…and he knew the voices. He was sure of it. But how…

In the next second, his thoughts were wiped from his head as two sets of feet dived, giggling, into the hut. Wrapped around each other, they faltered, clearly stunned at what they saw.

The old man screamed, 'Grab them!'

His body obeying, before his mind had caught up on events, Gisburne leapt to his feet. Wet clay dripped from his uniform, as he seized the girl.

Struggling like a trapped vixen in his arms, her yells rebounded off the stone walls, as the quarterstaff her companion held smacked into the old man's shoulder, knocking him onto the pile of clay—which reacted like a human in pain.

A shocked cry of 'Gulnar!!!!' rang from the big man's lips as he raised his staff upwards for a second time. 'Gisburne!!'

Gulnar?? Where do I know that name from? Gisburne froze, the struggling figure of Meg still in his arms, as he braced himself to be knocked to the floor. But a sound from outside stopped every single one of the cave's occupants in their tracks.

'Gisburne!! Where the hell are you?'

The outlaw blanched at the sound of the sheriff's voice, which sent him staggering back.

With a hushed promise of, 'I'll be back, Meg,', Little John ran out of the cave.

Gisburne stood motionless, the small woman still wriggling in his unwavering grasp. All he could see was the clay before him. It had hands, a face… and it was squirming against the cave floor.

'Put your hand over her mouth while I find some cloth.' Gulnar spoke with a calm assurance that belied the fact he'd just been floored with a blow from a deadly weapon. The expression on his waxen face chilled Gisburne to the bone.

Doing as he commanded, wincing as Meg bit into his palm in an attempt to escape, Gisburne's confused mind tried to work out of what was happening.

Gulnar? Why do I know that name? And who is this woman? Why does she know me?

As Gulnar came towards them, a coil of rope in his hands and a triumphant gleam to his eyes, Gisburne trembled almost as hard as Meg did. He could feel her lips trying to move behind his palm as the old man secured her hands behind her back, before kneeling to tether her ankles together. Working fast, the sorcerer produced a woollen rag, and had stuffed it between Meg's teeth the second Gisburne released his hold.

Only once Meg was lying on the floor—helpless next to the seething mound of clay—did Gisburne register the sweat that was pouring down his face. *I do know that woman… I knew the man … who are they?*

'This is better than I could have hoped.' Gulnar beamed at the angry, trapped, woman, who was battling against her bonds like a fly trapped in a spider's web. 'I thought she would turn and run, and that it would be the man who assisted us. While it would have been a fitting revenge to use one of *his* men against him, she is so much more… convenient; seeing as you only brought me a small amount of clay.'

Small amount? Gisburne's muscles ached from the cart load of clay he'd personally moved from the riverbank to the castle garden. *How can this not be enough?*

'A smaller figure to copy will help our cause.'

'Cause?'

He turned to face his helper. 'You have heard my name, and yet you still do not remember me, Sir Guy?'

'Remember…'

'We met, albeit briefly, at Huntingdon Castle. I'm sure, somewhere deep under my enchantment, your mind is telling you what I am.'

'Castle…' Gisburne blinked, as a vision of dancing flashed through his mind. 'Candles and a woman… Leaford… Huntingdon… Robert…' As the fragments of his mind came together, Gisburne whispered, 'Owen of Clun.'

'Well done. My master was Owen of Clun.' He kicked at Meg's foot, 'That prone creature's lover works for the man who destroyed him. And I will have my revenge. I *will*.'

'But… how… when…?'

'When?' Gulnar smiled, 'Sometime between now and forever.'

The second the sorcerer had spoken, Gisburne's uncertainty evaporated, and he smiled. 'And I will help you.'

'That's better.' Gulnar nodded. 'Now then, the clay senses us. It knows what I want of it—but more work needs to be done.'

'Yes.'

'Touch her face, Sir Guy, then touch the clay. It will know what to do.'

Obeying instantly, ignoring the stifled protests and the stream of angry tears on Meg's cheeks, Guy placed his palms on her face, and then onto the clay. What he saw made him draw back in horrified awe.

Oozing and spitting, the clay changed, moulding itself until, peering through brand-new, grey eyes, a replica of Meg of Wickham's face stared back up at him.

'It's her!'

'Almost.' Gulnar rubbed his hands together. 'Her, but not hers. She is mine. I shall steer her thoughts. Her mind is malleable as the clay that forms her.'

'I don't understand.'

'Because I do not wish you to.' Gulnar ran his hands over the length of the clay. 'When you are my son, you will know. And then you will walk willingly at my side with no need for incantations.'

'Your son?'

'There will be many sons, and they will howl to the moon. I have seen it.'

'I…'

Holding up a hand to silence his helper, Gulnar snapped. 'There will be time to explain later. Now, we need to hurry. It won't be long before that giant oaf returns to try and save the wench.'

An indignant squeak from Meg added wings to Gulnar's movements. 'Be silent, both of you. I need to concentrate.'

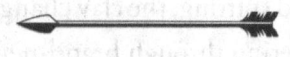

Gisburne brushed his hands together, sending little flakes of drying clay dancing around him. He wasn't sure how long he'd been helping Gulnar in the cave before he'd been instructed to leave, but he couldn't remember the last time he'd felt so satisfied after a hard day's work. It was fun moulding clay. *Perhaps I should leave the sheriff and become a potter?*

Hovering at the caves' mouth, his picturing of a happy life, coiling pots together while a wife and child watched him at work, faded.

'I told you to go!'

Gulnar's screech cut him to the bone.

Gisburne wasn't sure what he'd done wrong. *I was helping…. I was to be his son…*

'Hurry! Go!' Gulnar was hurrying around the cave, yelling over his shoulder as he worked. 'For now, your usefulness is over. The sheriff will need you and *you* will need him—I will see you again. I *will.*'

'But… when will…'

'Sometime between now and forever.'

Gisburne had only wandered a few yards across the overgrown garden, when he became aware of a tall man brandishing a quarterstaff towering over him.

Automatically reaching for his sword, Gisburne hesitated. Conflicting commands were somersaulting around his brain as the staff slammed against his fingers.

'Don't even think about it, Gisburne.' Little John growled. 'What's happening to Meg?'

'Meg?'

'Oh, for God's sake, Gisburne.' The sheriff peered around from behind the outlaw, who he was using as a human shield. He regarded his deputy with far more caution than he was showing the notorious felon. 'What has got into you?'

'Nothing. I'm...'

'It's not nothing!' John hissed; his eyes darting in every direction. 'Meg is in there with one of the wickedest men in the world and *you* are helping him!'

'Helping? ... I'm....' Gisburne's words constricted in his throat as his sight blurred for a moment. He looked from one of the men before him to the other. 'You two... you don't normally help each other... do you?'

'No, we do *not*!' The sheriff's response was fast.

Glaring at the sheriff, John barked under his

breath. 'Here and now we are helping each other, but just while you and Meg are in danger, Gisburne.'

'*Me* and Meg?'

Gisburne watched, baffled, as the sheriff took a reluctant step nearer to the bearded outlaw, whispering, 'You were right, he has been possessed.'

'Aye, and with that one in there, a simple knocking on the head isn't going to bring him out of it. Let's get him into the trees.'

Placidly letting himself be dragged under the cover of the woodland, Gisburne heard the big man say, 'If you betray me, sheriff, or if you do, Gisburne, then Robin will see you dead. Do you understand? Dead. Both of you.'

'You've made your point.' The sheriff snapped, as they came to a halt under a tangle of neglected branches. 'Why are you covered in clay, Gisburne, and what in Hell's name is Clun's sorcerer doing in one of my caves?!'

'Sorcerer?'

'Yes!'

'I'm helping the old man. I don't know about a sorcerer.'

'Gisburne, the only person you have ever helped in your whole life is yourself.' De Rainault prodded his deputy in the chest. 'Now talk to me.'

'I just got a hermit some water and herbs—oh, and some clay. That's all.'

John scowled, looking anxiously around him. 'Will you keep your voice down!?'

'If it will help,' Gisburne whispered.

Deciding he far preferred the unhelpful Gisburne to this placid version, John addressed the sheriff. 'The clay was moving.'

'Moving?' De Rainault's voice dripped scorn. 'You haven't been possessed as well, have you?'

'I tell you, Sheriff, that clay on the cave floor, it was moving like it were alive.'

As the giant's palm clenched his shoulder, Gisburne winced, and his gaze flickered back towards the cave and the castle garden. An inner terror, one that his brain had been stoically ignoring for some time, was growing fast. Licking his dry lips, he muttered, 'You... I have met you before somewhere.'

The sheriff rolled his eyes. 'Well done, Gisburne. Sharp as an arrow, as usual.'

'What does Gulnar want with Meg?' John kept a tight hold on Gisburne's sword arm, one eye on the sheriff, and the other on the cave, which he could just see through the mass of leaf-drenched branches.

'He's practising.'

'I beg your pardon?' The sheriff took a step back from his deputy.

'Revenge…' Gisburne's set smile faded a little, as fragments of the past few days swam around his mind. *Herbs… chanting… dancing red flames and the clay… moving clay…*

'But Meg hasn't done anything to him!' John spoke fast. 'It was bad enough when Gulnar tortured me with dreams of seeing her killed. Over and over I saw her, run down by…' he swung around, his stare fixed on the sheriff, '…*your* men. But the only thing Meg has ever done that could be seen as wrong in your eyes is love me, and I will not see her punished for that!'

'Meg of Wickham…' Gisburne mumbled, his forehead creasing in confusion.

'You do remember her, don't you, Gisburne?' Little John exchanged a worried look with the sheriff. 'She lives in Wickham, with Edward and the others.'

'Wickham? Trouble…we've had trouble there.' Gisburne muttered. The sheriff turned on him. 'Damn right we've had trouble there, Gisburne! *Him*, for a start.' The sheriff stabbed a sharp finger at Little John. 'Don't you remember, Gisburne? You've been humiliated in Wickham so many times that surely…'

'Humiliated…' Gisburne's eyes blazed, an intense anger paralysing him. Seething, he didn't notice John remove the sword from his belt before gripping his arms behind his back as he spat at his employer. '…That's what you do to me. That's why I was leaving… I *was* leaving….' His words faltered as his eyes blazed, his glare focused entirely on De Rainault's small figure. 'You threw wine at me and…. I went off to think. There was an old man who…'

'That was Gulnar!!'

A dreamy smile returned to Gisburne's voice as he said, 'Umm… yes. I'm his deputy now. I'm going to be his son.'

'His son?' The sheriff exchanged a wary look with Little John.

'One of his sons. He has seen it.'

John sucked on his bottom lip. 'Gulnar does see things. Worse, he can make *you* see things, like I said. Things that aren't real. And he *hates* Robin… If he is planning on making Gisburne his son, as the sort of opposite to Robin being Herne's Son…'

The sheriff shivered. 'That is a situation I do not want to consider.'

'Nor do I!' John fidgeted, 'I have to get Meg out of there. Or rather…' he gripped Gisburne by the collar and lifted him off his feet, and then growled at his bemused expression. '...*you* are going to go back in there and fetch her, Gisburne.'

'But Gulnar said not to come back.' Gisburne shrugged, a set smile coming back to his face. 'But I'll see him again. I'll be useful again.'

'You haven't been useful in years.'

'Shut up, sheriff.' John shifted his weight, taking a firmer hold of his adversary. 'If Gulnar has finished with Gisburne, here, then the enchantment might wear off soon.'

'I hope so! There's not much more of that smile I can take.' De Rainault groaned, 'Bloody sorcerers. At least when the Baron de Belleme was around, he had intelligence and breeding! This one's barking mad.'

'We have to get....' A movement from behind sent John into silence and he put his hand up to cover Gisburne's mouth. 'Shh... what was that noise?'

A muffled scream made all three men tense. Then, Gisburne found himself being abruptly dragged forward as the outlaw got as close to the edge of the thicket as he could.

The sound of a male cry of pain followed on the heels of a second scream, making John smile with pride. But the smile was short-lived, as a female's screech flew from the cave.

'We are going to get her. Now!'

'We? But Gisburne was going?' The sheriff sounded panicked.

'Look at him! He hasn't got a clue what's going on, and if it's all the same to you, sheriff, I'd rather not wait around for him to remember who I am or who he is.'

'I bet you wouldn't!'

Taking Gisburne's belt, John used it to secure the deputy's hands behind his back. 'Come on, Sheriff!'

Watching in bemusement, Gisburne saw his superior and the outlaw run to cave. He was going to call after them to ask if they wanted help, but they had already gone.

'Typical sheriff, he never appreciates my assistance.' Settling himself on the rough ground, Gisburne got as comfortable as possible, resting his back and tethered arms against a gnarled tree trunk, and closed his eyes. The sound of a bird singing filtered through the fog in his mind. *That sounds like a robin.*

A robin….

Gisburne sat forward. *I've forgotten something… something important. Something I can almost see and then…*

A crash of fallen pottery made Gisburne twist in

the direction of the cave. Seconds later a bellow of 'No…' rang through the air.

Instantly, Gisburne's body cramped in pain as he felt the intense depth of Gulnar's rage. The strangled, shrill scream of defeat filled him from the inside.

He's failed… it hasn't worked… the clay…

Bright red flames danced behind Gisburne's eyelids, as he sank to the brambled floor. As he lost consciousness, a defiant thought ricocheted through him:

We will meet again, when the sky cries out. We will meet again, sometime between now and forever…

'Manual labour!!' The sheriff crashed a goblet against the side of the able. 'That outlaw forced *me* to do manual labour!'

Wincing, Gisburne massaged his head as the sheriff's voice bounced across the otherwise empty hall.

'My cloak will never be the same again. That clay will never come out! The damn stuff was moving… I swear it tried to grab my ankles. And what did

Little John do? Help me? No! He just sat with that whinging woman of his, cradling her unconscious body until all the hard work was done!'

'Why are you talking into your goblet, my Lord.'

'Oh, Gisburne.' The sheriff looked startled and edged his seat a fraction away from the approaching deputy. 'Feeling better?'

Gisburne sank onto his seat. Taking a sip of claret, he wrinkled his nose and put it back onto the table. It didn't taste as good as he remembered.

'Are you listening to me, Gisburne?'

'Incessantly, my Lord.' He closed his eyes. *Wasn't I going to leave? Why didn't I go?* 'You were asking if I was better. My answer is no, I'm not. My head is killing me.'

'You've only yourself to blame, Gisburne. If you hadn't tried to run away from here, then…'

'I've told you before, I didn't run away, I just went into the garden to think and then I got talking to an old man, and…

'Someone must have knocked you out.'

Gisburne's eyes narrowed. 'Was it you, my Lord?'

'How dare you!?'

'You threw wine over me.' Gisburne snorted, 'If you hadn't, I wouldn't have gone outside.' Picking a strip of meat up off a platter, he chewed thoughtfully.

'I didn't know where I was when I came round. Not for a while. Why are the castle gardens such a mess?'

'Because I have more important things to worry about, Gisburne, than flora and fauna! There is a gang of cutthroats in the forest, remember!?'

'Of course I remember!'

'Have you had the cave sealed yet? The last thing I want is another hermit making his home there.'

'I oversaw the work myself.' Gisburne felt his stomach clench, as he remembered how nauseous he'd felt as a group of servants and men-at-arms had worked hard and fast, filling the cave's mouth with stones. 'No one could get in there now.'

'More importantly, Gisburne, no one can get out!' The sheriff took a slow sip of his wine.

'Before I was knocked out, I was going to suggest…'

De Rainault interrupted, 'Or fell over and knocked yourself out.'

Not caring for the odd way the sheriff was peering at him, Gisburne insisted, 'I was knocked out. I'm not clumsy.'

'If you say so, Gisburne. That makes you unobservant and lacking in a fighting instinct instead. Sounds about right.'

Slamming a palm against the table, Gisburne jumped to his feet. 'Do you want me to leave? Do you?'

'Oh sit down, Gisburne. What were you doing to suggest before you were knocked out?'

'I'd had an idea about the outlaws.'

'Really, Gisburne, go on. Amaze me.'

'Why don't you capture the outlaws by paying a sorcerer to enchant him to do your bidding, my Lord?'

The sheriff carefully lowered his goblet back to the table. 'Where did you get that idea from, Gisburne?'

'I don't know, my Lord. It just came to me.'

'Well, I'd let it go away again, if I were you. Magic is nothing but trouble…'

You may also enjoy…

You may also enjoy…